生活英語品萬用手冊

English
Conversation Skills

張瑜凌 ▶ 編著

Part 1
必備單字

Part 2
必備動詞

Part 3
好用動詞片語

目 錄 Contents

Part ④
常用生活用語

Part ⑤
基本句型

Part 6
道地俚語
(MP3)

Part 7
生活短語

Part 8
常用問句

MP3

Part

1

必備單字

用餐

▶ 一餐	meal
▶ 早餐	breakfast
▶ 午餐	lunch
▶ 晚餐	dinner
▶ 點心	snack
▶ 甜點	dessert
▶ 吃	eat
▶ 咬住	bite
▶ 嚼	chew
▶ 喝	drink
▶ 吸食	suck
▶ 吸啜	sip
▶ 聞味道	smell
▶ 吞嚥	swallow

實用例句一

▷ What do you want for breakfast?
你早餐想吃什麼？

實用例句二

▷ After dinner, we had ice cream for dessert.
吃過晚飯之後，我們吃冰淇淋作為甜點。

肉類

▶肉	meat
▶牛肉	beef
▶牛排	steak
▶羊肉	mutton
▶羊排	muttonchop
▶豬肉	pork
▶雞肉	chicken
▶火雞肉	turkey
▶肉排	chop
▶瘦肉	lean
▶肥肉	fat
▶火腿	ham
▶香腸	sausage
▶雞腿	drumstick

實用例句一

▷I don't eat meat.
我不吃肉。

實用例句二

▷Is it white meat or red meat?
這是白肉還是紅肉？

海產

▶ 海鮮	seafood
▶ 魚	fish
▶ 烏魚	mullet
▶ 鮭魚	salmon
▶ 沙丁魚	sardine
▶ 鱈魚	cod
▶ 章魚	octopus
▶ 烏賊	squid
▶ 蛤蜊	clam
▶ 淡菜	mussel
▶ 牡蠣	oyster
▶ 蝦	shrimp
▶ 龍蝦	lobster
▶ 螃蟹	crab

實用例句一

▷ How about seafood?
要不要(點)海鮮？

實用例句二

▷ I'm allergic to shrimp.
我對蝦子過敏。

蔬菜

▶ 紅蘿蔔	carrot
▶ 白蘿蔔	turnip
▶ 洋蔥	onion
▶ 馬鈴薯	potato(複數 potatoes)
▶ 包心菜	cabbage
▶ 花椰菜	cauliflower
▶ 芹菜	celery
▶ 萵苣	lettuce
▶ 南瓜	pumpkin
▶ 玉米	corn
▶ 豌豆	pea
▶ 竹筍	bamboo
▶ 蕃茄	tomato(複數 tomatoes)
▶ 香菇	mushroom

實用例句一

▷ I always cry when I'm chopping onions.
我切洋蔥的時候總是會哭。

實用例句二

▷ I'd like to order pea soup.
我要點豌豆湯。

水果

▶ 蘋果	apple
▶ 梨子	pear
▶ 桃子	peach(複數 peaches)
▶ 奇異果	kiwi
▶ 香橙	orange
▶ 香蕉	banana
▶ 草莓	strawberry (複數 strawberries)
▶ 葡萄	grape
▶ 檸檬	lemon
▶ 櫻桃	cherry(複數 cherries)
▶ 木瓜	papaya
▶ 椰子	coconut
▶ 胡桃	walnut
▶ 杏仁	almond

實用例句一

▷His job was to peel apples.
他的工作是削蘋果皮。

實用例句二

▷I will buy a bunch of bananas.
我要買一串香蕉。

飲料

▶ 飲料	drinks
▶ 冷飲	cold drinks
▶ 飲料	beverage
▶ 酒精飲料	alcohol
▶ 水	water
▶ 礦泉水	mineral water
▶ 茶	tea
▶ 紅茶	black tea
▶ 冰紅茶	iced black tea
▶ 果汁	juice
▶ 蘋果汁	apple juice
▶ 柳橙汁	orange juice
▶ 檸檬汁	lemonade
▶ 咖啡	coffee
▶ 葡萄酒	wine

實用例句一

▷ May I have a glass of water?
可以給我一杯水嗎？

實用例句二

▷ Make me a cup of coffee.
幫我泡一杯咖啡。

西式點心

▶ 巧克力	chocolate
▶ 餅乾	cookie
▶ 麵包	bread
▶ 蛋糕	cake
▶ 糖果	candy(複數 candies)
▶ 熱狗	hot dog
▶ 甜甜圈	doughnut
▶ 披薩	pizza
▶ 洋蔥圈	onion ring
▶ 爆米花	popcorn
▶ 洋芋片	potato chips
▶ 優格	yogurt
▶ 冰淇淋	ice cream
▶ 布丁	pudding

實用例句一

▷ I took her a box of chocolates.
我帶給她一盒巧克力了。

實用例句二

▷ I only had a yogurt for lunch.
我只有吃一份優格當午餐。

餐具

▶餐刀	knife
▶牛排刀	steak knife
▶叉子	fork
▶碗	bowl
▶筷子	chopsticks
▶盤子	dish
▶湯匙	spoon
▶咖啡壺	coffeepot
▶杯了	cup
▶咖啡杯	coffee cup
▶水杯	glass
▶酒杯	wineglass
▶茶壺	teapot
▶罐、壺	pitcher

實用例句一

▷ Would you like a cup of coffee?
你要喝杯咖啡嗎？

實用例句二

▷ Two glasses of lemonade, please.
(我要點)兩杯檸檬汁，謝謝！

計量單位

▶ 一袋豆子	a bag of beans
▶ 一束玫瑰	a bouquet of roses
▶ 一箱蘋果	a box of apples
▶ 一串葡萄	a bunch of grapes
▶ 一束玉米	a sheaf of corn
▶ 一塊條型巧克力	a bar of chocolate
▶ 一罐起司	a can of cheese
▶ 一瓶蕃茄醬	a bottle of ketchup
▶ 一盒菸	a carton of cigarettes
▶ 一打蛋	a dozen of eggs
▶ 一盎司的巧克力脆片	
	an ounce of chocolate chips
▶ 一夸脫油	a quart of oil
▶ 一加侖牛奶	a gallon of milk
▶ 一磅砂糖	a pound of sugar
▶ 一條麵包	a loaf of bread
▶ 一段口香糖	a stick of chewing gum
▶ 一串香蕉	a hand of bananas
▶ 一杯水	a glass of water
▶ 少量的鹽	a tad of salt
▶ 一點檸檬	a bit of lemon
▶ 一片派	a piece of the pie

▶ 一把剪刀	a pair of scissors
▶ 一雙短襪	a pair of socks
▶ 一張紙	a sheet of paper
▶ 一件家俱	a piece of furniture
▶ 一片麵包	a piece of bread
▶ 一根粉筆	a piece of chalk
▶ 一條線	a piece of string
▶ 一座大砲	a piece of ordnance
▶ 一幅畫	a piece of painting
▶ 幾則忠告	several pieces of advice
▶ 一樁愚蠢的行為	a piece of folly
▶ 一件幸運的事	a piece of good luck
▶ 一拋屎	a piece of shit

實用例句一

▷ There are 16 ounces in one pound.
一磅有十六盎司。

實用例句二

▷ Two loaves of white bread, please.
(我要買)兩條白麵包,謝謝!

服裝

▶衣服	clothes
▶服裝	dress
▶燕尾服	tailcoat
▶大衣	coat
▶外套	jacket
▶休閒服	casual clothes
▶短袖圓領衫	T-shirt
▶牛仔裝	jeans
▶男裝	suit
▶西裝	business suit
▶棒球外套	bomber
▶襯衫	shirt
▶褲子	pants
▶領帶	tie
▶袖扣	cuff link
▶女用襯衫	blouse
▶洋裝	dress
▶裙子	skirt
▶迷你裙	miniskirt
▶窄裙	slim skirt
▶胸罩	bra
▶泳衣	swimwear
▶比基尼泳衣	bikini

飾品

▶珠寶	jewelry
▶珍珠	pearl
▶鑽石	diamond
▶黃金	gold
▶玉	jade
▶紅寶石	carbuncle
▶藍寶石	sapphire
▶胸針	brooch
▶別針	pin
▶耳環	earring
▶項鍊	necklace
▶手鐲	bracelet
▶戒指	ring

實用例句一

▷ This is a piece of silver jewelry.
這是一件銀首飾。

實用例句二

▷ He was wearing an earring in his left ear.
他在他的左耳戴了一個耳環。

褲子

▶長褲	pants
▶打摺褲	pleated front pants
▶緊身喇叭褲	loon pants
▶平口褲	flat front pants
▶防皺褲	wrinkle-free pants
▶寬管褲	wide leg pants
▶喇叭褲	bell-bottoms
▶運動褲	sport pants
▶農夫褲	crop pants
▶無腰身褲	no-waist pants
▶五分褲	knee shorts
▶短褲	short trousers
▶馬褲	breeches

實用例句一

▷ I'd need a pair of white pants.
我會需要一件白色的褲子。

實用例句二

▷ Your belt goes just right with your blue pants.
你的腰帶正好配你的藍色褲子。

個人物品

▶ 眼鏡	glasses
▶ 太陽眼鏡	sunglasses
▶ 隱形眼鏡	contact lens
▶ 手錶	watch(複數 watches)
▶ 雨傘	umbrella
▶ 小型手提箱	briefcase
▶ 袋子	bag
▶ 背包	backpack
▶ 錢包	purse
▶ 皮夾	wallet
▶ 手提包	handbag
▶ 背包	knapsack
▶ 手提箱	suitcase

實用例句一

▷ I will buy a pair of glasses.
　我要買一副眼鏡。

實用例句二

▷ I left my wallet in a taxi.
　我把我的錢包遺忘在計程車上了。

鞋襪

▶ 短襪	socks
▶ 長襪	stockings
▶ 絲襪	silk stockings
▶ 毛襪	woolen stockings
▶ 鞋子	shoes
▶ 高跟鞋	high-heeled shoes
▶ 平底鞋	flat-heeled shoes
▶ 運動鞋	sports shoes
▶ 跑步鞋	running shoes
▶ 網球鞋	tennis shoes
▶ 橡皮底帆布鞋	sneaker
▶ 靴子	boots
▶ 拖鞋	slippers
▶ 涼鞋	sandals

實用例句一

▷ Put on your shoes and socks.
穿上你的鞋襪。

實用例句二

▷ He took off his new pair of shoes.
他脫下他的新鞋子。

顏色

▶ 顏色	color
▶ 白色	white
▶ 灰色	gray
▶ 銀色	silver
▶ 紅色	red
▶ 粉紅色	pink
▶ 橙色	orange
▶ 棕色	brown
▶ 黃色	yellow
▶ 黑色	black
▶ 金色	gold
▶ 綠色	green
▶ 藍色	blue
▶ 紫色	purple

實用例句一

▷ What color are your eyes?
你的眼睛是什麼顏色？

實用例句二

▷ Does the skirt come in red?
這件裙子有紅色的嗎？

房屋

▶房子	house
▶公寓	apartment
▶套房	suite
▶分層的公寓	flat
▶透天房屋	townhouse
▶建築物	building
▶宿舍	dormitory
▶摩天樓	skyscraper
▶(農舍式的)小別墅	cottage
▶別墅	country house
▶莊園	estate
▶避暑別墅	summer house
▶社區	community
▶城堡	castle

實用例句一

▷ I'm going to buy a house.
我要買房子。

實用例句二

▷ What a tall building.
好高的建築物！

房間

▶ 房間	room
▶ 門廊	lobby
▶ 客廳	living room
▶ 衣櫃間	walk-in closet
▶ 餐廳	dining room
▶ 臥室	bedroom
▶ 客房	guest room
▶ 廚房	kitchen
▶ 浴廁	bathroom
▶ 車庫	garage
▶ 庭院	garden
▶ 閣樓	attic
▶ 儲藏室	storeroom
▶ 地下室	basement

實用例句一

▷ She's waiting for you in the conference room.
她正在會議室裡等你。

實用例句二

▷ The house has a large garden.
這間房子有大庭院。

傢俱

▶ 傢俱	furniture
▶ 桌子	table
▶ 沙發	sofa
▶ 躺椅	couch
▶ 坐臥兩用椅	recliner
▶ 桌子	table
▶ 茶几	coffee table
▶ 凳子	stool
▶ 高腳椅	high chair
▶ 長凳	bench
▶ 高背椅	settle
▶ 碗櫥	cupboard
▶ 床	bed
▶ 臥房用衣櫃	bureau
▶ 櫃子	cabinet
▶ 書櫃	bookshelf

實用例句一

▷ They have a lot of antique furniture.
他們有很多古董家俱。

實用例句二

▷ He likes to have breakfast in bed.
他喜歡在床上吃早餐。

日常用品

▶物品	stuff
▶垃圾桶	garbage can
▶花瓶	vase
▶古董	antique
▶檯燈	lamp
▶日光燈管	fluorescent tube
▶燈泡	light bulb
▶手電筒	flashlight
▶遙控器	remote control
▶溫度計	thermometer
▶煙灰缸	ashtray
▶殺蟲劑	pesticide
▶電池	battery(複數 batteries)
▶急救箱	emergency box

實用例句一

▷ There's sticky stuff all over the chair.
椅子上到處都是黏呼呼的東西。

實用例句二

▷ Do you see that street lamp?
你有看見那個街燈嗎？

家用電器

▶ 電視機	TV set
▶ 錄放影機	VCR
▶ 音響	stereo
▶ 收音機	radio
▶ 錄音機	tape recorder
▶ 傳真機	fax machine
▶ 電話	telephone
▶ 中央空調	central air-conditioning
▶ 電熱器	electric heater
▶ 暖氣機	heater
▶ 風扇	fan
▶ 空氣清淨機	air cleaner
▶ 冷氣機	air conditioner
▶ 割草機	lawn mower

實用例句一

▷ The concert will be broadcast in stereo.
演唱會將由立體音響播放。

實用例句二

▷ I like to listen to the radio.
我喜歡聽收音機。

親屬

▶祖父	grandfather
▶祖母	grandmother
▶父親	father
▶母親	mother
▶公公、岳父	father-in-law
▶婆婆、岳母	mother-in-law
▶伯/叔/舅父	uncle
▶伯/叔/舅母	aunt
▶女婿	son-in-law
▶媳婦	daughter-in-law
▶丈夫	husband
▶妻子	wife
▶姊/妹夫	brother-in-law
▶姑/嫂	sister-in-law
▶兄弟	brother
▶姐妹	sister
▶堂(表)兄妹	cousin
▶兒子	son
▶女兒	daughter
▶外甥、姪兒	nephew
▶甥女、姪女	niece
▶孫子	grandson
▶孫女	granddaughter

家庭生活

▶做家事	do the housework
▶熨燙衣服	do the ironing
▶清潔	do the cleaning
▶洗碗	do the dishes
▶做飯	do the cooking
▶做午餐	do lunch
▶做晚餐	do dinner
▶逛街	do the shopping
▶做飯	make dinner
▶沏茶	make tea
▶生火	make a fire
▶整理床鋪	make the bed
▶淋浴	take a shower
▶洗澡	have a bath

實用例句一

▷ Will you do the dishes?
你會洗碗嗎？

實用例句二

▷ Please make a cup of tea for me.
幫我泡一杯茶。

行動

▶走路	walk
▶漫步	wander
▶跳躍	jump
▶滑倒	slip
▶絆倒	trip
▶跌倒	fall
▶跑步	run
▶去	go
▶旅行	travel
▶騎乘(馬、自行車、公車)	ride
▶駕駛	drive
▶飛翔	fly
▶乘火車	ride in a train
▶騎腳踏車	ride on a bicycle
▶騎在馬背上	ride on horseback
▶上(船、機車)	come aboard
▶航程	flight

實用例句一

▷I walked home.
我走路回家的。

實用例句二

▷I fell down the stairs and injured my back.
我從樓梯摔下弄傷我的背了。

捷運、火車、地鐵

▶捷運	metro
▶火車	train
▶地鐵	subway
▶電車	trolley
▶車廂	box car
▶時刻表	timetable
▶到站停止	stop
▶站別	station
▶月臺	platform
▶入口	entrance
▶出口	exit
▶地圖	map
▶票價	fare

實用例句一

▷ Where is the train station?
　火車站在哪裡？

實用例句二

▷ Do you have any maps of this city?
　你有這個城市的地圖嗎？

計程車、公車

▶ 乘客	passenger
▶ 司機	driver
▶ 計程車費	taxi fare
▶ 計程車	taxi
▶ 公共汽車	bus
▶ 到達	arrive
▶ 起程	depart
▶ 離開	leave
▶ 路線	route
▶ 公共汽車站	bus station
▶ 計程車招呼站	taxi station
▶ 車票	ticket

實用例句一

▷ Call me a taxi, please.
請幫我叫部計程車。

實用例句二

▷ I live on a bus route so I can easily get to work.
公車路線有經過我家，所以我能很容易去上班。

數字

▶ 一	one
▶ 二	two
▶ 三	three
▶ 四	four
▶ 五	five
▶ 六	six
▶ 七	seven
▶ 八	eight
▶ 九	nine
▶ 十	ten
▶ 十一	eleven
▶ 十二	twelve
▶ 十三	thirteen
▶ 十四	fourteen
▶ 十五	fifteen
▶ 十六	sixteen
▶ 十七	seventeen
▶ 十八	eighteen
▶ 十九	nineteen
▶ 廿	twenty
▶ 廿五	twenty-five
▶ 卅	thirty
▶ 四十	forty

▶四十三	forty-three
▶五十	fifty
▶六十	sixty
▶七十	seventy
▶八十	eighty
▶九十	ninety
▶一百	a hundred
▶一千	a thousand
▶一萬	ten thousand
▶十萬	one hundred thousand
▶一百萬	a million
▶千萬	ten million
▶一億	a hundred million
▶十億	billion

時間

▶世紀	century
▶年	year
▶月份	month
▶日子	day
▶日期	date
▶時間	time
▶鐘點	o'clock
▶小時	hour
▶分鐘	minute
▶秒鐘	second
▶快的	fast
▶慢的	slow
▶晚的	late
▶提早的	early

實用例句一

▷ What's the time?
幾點鐘？

實用例句二

▷ She's a very slow eater.
她吃得非常慢。

星期

▶ 星期	week
▶ 週末	weekend
▶ 平日	weekday
▶ 星期一	Monday(縮寫 Mon.)
▶ 星期二	Tuesday(縮寫 Tue.)
▶ 星期三	Wednesday(縮寫 Wed.)
▶ 星期四	Thursday(縮寫 Thu.)
▶ 星期五	Friday(縮寫 Fri.)
▶ 星期六	Saturday(縮寫 Sat.)
▶ 星期日	Sunday(縮寫 Sun.)

實用例句一

▷ We go to the cinema about once a week.
我們大約一星期去一次戲院。

實用例句二

▷ I start my new job on Monday.
我在星期一開始我的新工作。

月份

▶一月	January (縮寫 Jan.)
▶二月	February(縮寫 Feb.)
▶三月	March(縮寫 Mar.)
▶四月	April(縮寫 Apr.)
▶五月	May
▶六月	June(縮寫 Jun.)
▶七月	July(縮寫 Jul.)
▶八月	August(縮寫 Aug.)
▶九月	September(縮寫 Sept.)
▶十月	October(縮寫 Oct.)
▶十一月	November(縮寫 Nov.)
▶十二月	December(縮寫 Dec.)

實用例句一

▷ My mother's birthday is in May.
我母親的生日是在五月。

實用例句二

▷ We're leaving for France on September ninth.
我們九月九日要出發去法國。

★行動學習系列 03★

公共場所

▶商店	shop
▶商店	store
▶市場	market
▶超級市場	supermarket
▶食品雜貨店	grocery
▶跳蚤市場	flea market
▶旅館	hotel
▶汽車旅館	motcl
▶餐廳	restaurant
▶酒吧	bar
▶酒館、酒店	pub
▶咖啡館	cafe
▶銀行	bank
▶郵局	post office
▶法院	court
▶車站	station
▶機場	airport
▶港口	port
▶停車場	parking lot
▶加油站	gas station
▶教堂	church
▶醫院	hospital
▶圖書館	library

▶博物館	museum
▶美術館	art gallery
▶電影院	cinema
▶劇院	theater
▶俱樂部	club
▶體育館	gym
▶公園	park
▶動物園	zoo
▶學校	school
▶大學	university
▶學院	college
▶高中	senior high school
▶國中	junior high school
▶小學	primary school
▶幼稚園	kindergarten

實用例句一

▷ I noticed him going into the hotel bar.
　我注意到了他進去旅館的酒吧中。

實用例句二

▷ We're building a new school in the village.
　我們正在村莊中興建一所學校。

Part

2

必備動詞

like
喜歡

▷I like it.
我喜歡它。

▷I like that.
我喜歡那個。

▷I like this.
我喜歡這個。

▷I like that guy.
我喜歡那個傢伙。

▷I like him.
我喜歡他。

▷I don't like her.
我不喜歡她。

▷We don't like your ideas.
我們不喜歡你的主意。

▷She likes it, and so do I.
她喜歡它,我也是(喜歡它)。

▷She doesn't like this dress.
她不喜歡這件衣服。

▷John doesn't like swimming.
約翰不喜歡游泳。

▷Do you like it?
你喜歡它嗎?

▷How do you like it?
你有多喜歡它?

▷My son would have liked it!
我兒子一定會很喜歡它。

▷She's so cute and I like her shirt.
她真是可愛,而我喜歡她的襯衫。

try
嘗試、努力、試驗

▷ Try again.
再試一次。

▷ Try harder.
多努力嘗試。

▷ Try to get it.
試著去得到。

▷ Try me.
說來聽聽。

▷ Try to be there on time.
試著準時到達那裡。

▷ Try not to be late.
試著不要遲到。

▷ I try to open my eyes wider.
我嘗試把我的眼睛睜開一點。

▷ I tried to open the window.
我有試著打開窗戶。

▷ I'd love to try that.
我願意嘗試看看。

▷ I've tried everything.
所有的方法我都已經試過了。

▷ I've tried really hard.
我已經非常努力試過了。

▷ I'll try again next year.
明年我會再試一次。

▷ Perhaps you should try getting up earlier.
也許你應該早一點起床。

▷ Keep trying and you'll find a job eventually.
繼續努力，你終究會找到工作的。

do

做、執行、行動、完成、扮演

▷ Do something.
想想辦法吧!

▷ Do me a favor, please.
請幫我一個忙。

▷ You did me a great favor.
你幫了我一個大忙。

▷ David is doing biophysics.
大衛在學習生物物理。

▷ What are you doing?
你正在做什麼?

▷ What did you do?
你做了什麼?

▷ Why did you do this to me?
為什麼你對我做了這件事?

▷ My mother does the cooking.
我母親在做飯。

▷ My son does well in school.
我兒子在校學業很好。

▷ I have done a lot of work.
我做了許多工作。

▷ Did you do your homework?
你有做功課了嗎?

▷ We tried to do a group shot of the kids.
我們試著要幫孩子們拍團體照。

▷ It's a pleasure to do business with you.
真高興和你做生意。

▷ Don't do anything stupid.
不要做傻事。

go
去、行走、進行、離去

▷ I go to work immediately.
我馬上就去上班。

▷ I am going to buy some apples.
我正要去買一些蘋果。

▷ I don't want to go with you.
我不想要和你一起去。

▷ We went to visit her parents.
我們去拜訪了她的父母。

▷ We went over to Maple Park.
我們去了楓葉公園。

▷ We went to New York for two days.
我們去了紐約兩天。

▷ He went to New York for a job interview.
他去了紐約面試。

▷ Let's not go this way.
我們不要走那一條路。

▷ May I go to the restroom?
我要去洗手間。

▷ Where are you going?
你正要去哪裡？

▷ Where do you want to go?
你想要去哪裡？

▷ When did she go?
她什麼時候離開的？

▷ We went by train.
我們是搭火車去的。

▷ Everything is going well.
一切都很順利。

come
回來、過來

▷ I came back at 5 P.M.
我下午五點回來的。

▷ You can come here to take your ticket.
你可以過來取你的票。

▷ Could you come to see me tomorrow?
明天你能來看我嗎？

▷ Come here and look at the picture.
過來看看這幅畫。

▷ Will you come with me to the store?
你會和我一道去商店嗎？

▷ When did you come home?
你什麼時候回家的？

▷ My sister is coming to the U.S.A.
我的姊妹要來美國。

▷ My parents are coming for dinner.
我的父母要過來吃晚餐。

▷ When do you want to come back?
你想要什麼時候回去？

▷ It was good of you to come and visit me.
有你來拜訪我真好。

▷ Please come in.
請進。

▷ May I come in?
我可以進來嗎？

▷ He won't be able to come.
他將無法回來。

▷ She will come and help you in a moment.
她會馬上過來幫你。

get
得到、買、理解、趕上搭乘、接通

▷ I got a letter yesterday.
我昨天收到一封信。

▷ I got a coat in that store yesterday.
昨天我在那家店買了一件外套。

▷ I'll get it for you.
我來幫你拿。

▷ I'll get him for you.
我來幫你叫他。

▷ I'll get you something to eat.
我來給你弄點吃的。

▷ I didn't get any answer from him.
我沒有得到他的任何答覆。

▷ How did you get this?
你怎麼拿到這個的？

▷ Let's get back to the starting point.
我們回到起點吧。

▷ Don't get me wrong.
不要誤會我的意思。

▷ I must get the one o'clock plane.
我一定要趕上一點的飛機。

▷ Could you get me Seattle, please?
請幫我接通西雅圖。

▷ Get out of here!
滾遠一點！

▷ What did you get from her?
你從她那裡得到了什麼？

▷ I've got an idea.
我有一個辦法了。

give
送、給予、提供、做(動作)、傳染(疾病)

▷ I won't give up.
我不會放棄的。

▷ I'll give it a wash.
我要把它洗一洗。

▷ Let's give him a hand.
我們來幫他吧!

▷ What would you like to give me?
你要給我什麼?

▷ I'd give her another change.
我會再給她另一個機會。

▷ I gave him a pen.
我給了他一枝筆。

▷ I give him a kiss on the forehead.
我在他的額頭上親了一下。

▷ Give me a break.
饒了我吧!

▷ Give me five.
來,擊掌吧!

▷ Give me your book.
給我你的書。

▷ Give me a second.
等我一下。

▷ Give me some change.
給我一些零錢。

▷ Give me a hand, please?
請幫我一下好嗎?

▷ My wife gave me the flu.
我太太把流感傳給我了。

take

拿、帶領、乘車、吃飯／藥、喝水、花費

▷ I took it to Maria.
我拿給了瑪莉亞。

▷ I took a book to David.
我拿了一本書給大衛。

▷ I took David to the zoo yesterday.
昨天我帶大衛去了動物園。

▷ We took the boys down to Arizona.
我們帶男孩們南下到了亞利桑那州。

▷ I took a shower after breakfast.
我早餐後有沖澡了。

▷ He took a bath after work.
下班後他洗了個澡。

▷ The flight will take three hours.
航程要飛三小時。

▷ Let's take a walk.
我們去散步吧！

▷ Remember to take the medicine.
記得要吃藥。

▷ It'll take me two hours to be there.
到那裡將會花我兩個小時的時間。

▷ I need to take your temperature.
我需要量你的體溫。

▷ We are taking a four-day trip to Seattle.
我們要花四天的旅程到西雅圖去。

▷ I'll take it.
我要買。/我要這個。

▷ I took a sick leave today.
我今天有請了病假。

make
製造、生產、烹調

▷ She made a cake.
她做了一個蛋糕。

▷ Did you make this dress or buy it?
這件衣服是你訂做的還是買(現成品)的？

▷ They are making a lot of noise.
他們製造了很多噪音。

▷ He's always making trouble.
他總是製造很多麻煩。

▷ The table is made of wood.
這張桌子是木頭做的。

▷ This car was made in the USA.
這輛車子是美國製造的。

▷ Will you make me a cup of coffee?
你可以幫我煮一杯咖啡嗎？

▷ Can you make a sandwich for me?
你可以幫我做一個三明治嗎？

▷ I think you've made a mistake.
我認為你犯了一個錯誤。

▷ I have made a reservation.
我已經有預約了。

▷ I made an appointment to see a doctor.
我預約了要看醫生。

▷ Where could I make a phone call?
我可以在哪裡打電話？

▷ How to make a kite?
要如何製作風箏？

▷ Do you know how to make a doll?
你知道要如何製作洋娃娃嗎？

have
擁有、體驗、生育、不得不

▷ I have an idea.
我有一個主意。

▷ Do you have any questions?
你有任何問題嗎？

▷ OK, let me have a look.
好的，讓我看一看。

▷ I'll have time to visit you on Monday.
星期一我有空的話，會去拜訪你。

▷ This coat has no pockets.
這件衣服沒有口袋。

▷ I had a good time.
我玩得高興極了。

▷ I had a wonderful time on the beach.
我在海灘上坑得尚興極了。

▷ They had their lunch in a cafeteria.
他們在一家自助餐廳吃了他們的午飯。

▷ Have fun, kids.
孩子們，好好玩吧！

▷ Have a cup of coffee, please.
請喝杯咖啡。

▷ I'll have New York Steak.
我要(點)紐約牛排。

▷ What would you like to have?
你要點什麼(餐點)？

▷ My wife is going to have a baby.
我妻子快要生孩子了。

▷ I have to go right now.
我得馬上就去。

turn

旋轉、翻轉、使轉向、放置、拐過

▷ I turned the key in the lock.
我在鑰匙孔內轉動鑰匙。

▷ She turned over and went to sleep.
她轉過身去睡覺。

▷ Turn around.
轉過身。

▷ Turn on the light.
打開電燈。

▷ Turn off the light.
關掉電燈。

▷ Turn to page 16.
翻到第16頁。

▷ He turned the page of the book.
他翻書的頁次。

▷ I sneeze and my eyes turn into itchy.
我打噴嚏然後我的眼睛就變得很癢。

▷ He turned his face to the wall.
他轉過臉面向牆壁。

▷ He turned the glass upside down.
他將玻璃杯子倒置。

▷ She turned back the sheets.
她將這張紙翻面。

▷ Should I turn right now?
我要現在右轉嗎？

▷ Turn right at the end of the street.
在這條街的盡頭處右轉。

▷ The bus turned into the hotel entrance.
公車繞進飯店的入口處。

call

叫喊、稱呼、叫醒、致電、召開會議

▷ He called the names of everyone in the class.
他在班上點名。

▷ We call him David.
我們叫他大衛。

▷ He called me over to his desk.
他把我叫到了他桌前。

▷ Just call me David.
叫我大衛就好。

▷ Call me a cab, please.
請幫我叫一部計程車。

▷ I called a cab for Mrs. Smith.
我幫史密斯太太叫一部計程車。

▷ Shall I call you a taxi?
我幫你叫部計程車好嗎？

▷ I will go and call him.
我去叫他。

▷ I call David on my cellular phone.
我用我的手機打電話給大衛。

▷ Did anyone call today?
今天有人打過電話來嗎？

▷ Call me at 86473663.
打電話到 86473663 給我。

▷ Call me at my office tomorrow.
明天打電話到我的辦公室給我。

▷ We called a meeting yesterday.
我們昨天有召開了會議。

▷ Please call me at eight A.M.
請在早上八點叫醒我。

answer
回答、回應、接電話

▷ Answer me.
回答我！

▷ Why didn't you answer me?
你為什麼沒有回答我？

▷ David didn't answer my questions.
大衛沒有回答我的問題。

▷ Did you answer my question?
你有回答我的問題嗎？

▷ "I don't know." she answered.
她回答：「我不知道。」

▷ I won't answer your question.
我不會回答你的問題。

▷ I did my best to answer his questions.
我有盡量回答他的問題。

▷ He answered that he didn't know.
他有回答表示不知道。

▷ He answered that he was wrong.
他有回答表示他錯了。

▷ Who answered the telephone?
是誰接的電話？

▷ Aren't you ganna answer it?
你沒有要接電話嗎？

▷ I knocked but no one answered.
我敲了門，但無人應答。

▷ We won't answer your questions.
我們將不會回答你的問題。

▷ I didn't answer my cellular phone.
我沒有接聽我的手機。

keep

擁有、保存、整理、遵守、防止、使保持

▷ Let's keep in touch.
我們要保持聯絡喔！

▷ Keep it safe.
要保持安全。

▷ Keep it simple.
要維持簡單。

▷ Keep it secret.
要保守秘密。

▷ Keep cool.
要保持冷靜。

▷ She kept crying.
她一直哭個不停。

▷ Try to keep at home.
試著待在家裡不要出門。

▷ Just keep yourself warm.
讓你自己保持溫暖。

▷ Where do you keep?
你住在哪裡？

▷ You may keep this book.
你可以留著這本書。

▷ This garden is always kept well.
這花園一直整理得很好。

▷ I keep my shoes from getting wet.
我保持不要弄濕鞋子。

▷ Keep away from the dog.
別靠近那隻狗。

▷ What kept you away last night?
你昨晚因為什麼事而無法來？

think

認為、思索、理解、預料

▷ What do you think?
你認為呢？

▷ What makes you think so?
你為什麼會這麼認為？

▷ I don't think so.
我不這麼認為。

▷ I think you're right.
我認為你是對的。

▷ I think he will come.
我想他會來的。

▷ I'll think about it.
我會考慮考慮。

▷ I can't think what you mean.
我不懂你是什麼意思。

▷ I didn't think to lend you money.
我沒想到要借你錢。

▷ Don't you think they are so cute?
你不覺得他們很可愛嗎？

▷ What are you thinking about?
你有什麼打算？

▷ I think, I'm just so good at it.
我覺得這一點我很厲害。

▷ I think I really shouldn't be doing this.
我覺得我真的不應該去做這件事。

▷ I think that I am right!
我認為我是對的。

▷ I think that I'll figure out what to do.
我覺得我會理解出來該做什麼。

want

想要、希望、需要、想見、要求

▷ I want it now!
我現在就想要。

▷ I want to be a good person.
我想要成為一個好人。

▷ I want to go home.
我想要回家。

▷ I want to say thank you.
我想要向你說聲謝謝。

▷ I want to get a closer look.
我想要近一點看看。

▷ David wants to join us.
大衛想要加入我們。

▷ Do you want to come over?
你要過來嗎？

▷ I don't want to buy it.
我不想要買。

▷ What do you want?
你想要幹嘛？

▷ What do you want from me?
你想要我幹嘛？

▷ Do you want it back?
你要拿回去嗎？

▷ I want you to come back.
我想要你回來。

▷ I really don't want Harry to die.
我真的不希望哈利死。

▷ I want to let the children do it.
我想要讓孩子們去做。

need
需要、必需

▷ I need you to come pick me up.
我需要你來接我。

▷ I need you to take care of your sister.
我需要你照顧你妹妹。

▷ I need to catch my train.
我需要去趕搭我的火車。

▷ I need to be there on time.
我需要準時到達那裡。

▷ You need to take a vacation.
你需要休假。

▷ I don't think you need to worry about this.
我認為你不必為這事擔心。

▷ David needs our help.
大衛需要我們的幫助。

▷ I need your help.
我需要你的幫助。

▷ I need your advice.
我需要你的建議。

▷ I don't need your advice.
我不需要你的建議。

▷ What do you need?
你需要什麼？

▷ Why should I need her money?
為什麼我應該會需要她的錢？

▷ Do you need a magazine?
你需要雜誌嗎？

▷ Do you need any help?
你需要幫助嗎？

tell

告知、告訴

▷ Let me tell you something.
讓我告訴你一些事情。

▷ He told me a story.
他告訴了我一個故事。

▷ I tell him a story before he goes to bed.
我總是在他睡覺前説故事給他聽。

▷ Why didn't you tell me?
你為什麼不告訴我？

▷ Did you tell the truth?
你有説出了事實嗎？

▷ Tell me about your family.
談一談有關你家人的事。

▷ Tell me all about your new job.
告訴我有關你的新工作。

▷ David told me he'd seen you in town.
大衛告訴我他有在城裡見過你了。

▷ Could you tell me when it will be ready?
你可以告訴我什麼時候會準備好嗎？

▷ I'll tell you what-let's go out for a drink.
聽好，我們去喝一杯！

▷ Don't tell me you've done this again.
不要説你又做了一次。

▷ I can tell she sees nothing.
我看得出來她什麼都不瞭解。

▷ It's so dark I couldn't tell it was you.
這麼暗我分辨不出來是你！

▷ He's good at telling jokes.
他很擅長説故事。

say

講、念、說話、表明、假定、認為

▷ What did you say?
你說什麼？

▷ What would you like to say?
你想要說什麼？

▷ "What did you say?" I said.
我說，「你剛剛說什麼？」

▷ "CJ, I love you." I said.
我說，「CJ，我愛你。」

▷ Say no more.
給點建議啊！

▷ Who can say?
我不知道。／誰又知道？

▷ You must learn to say "please."
你要學習說「請」。

▷ I said to myself "I was wondering."
我告訴我自己「我懷疑」。

▷ Don't believe anything he says.
不要相信他說的任何話。

▷ David says he is hungry.
大衛說他餓了。

▷ I'd rather not say.
我不想說。

▷ I would say so.
我是這麼認為的。

▷ They say it's raining now.
他們說現在正在下雨。

▷ Can you come to dinner? Let's say 5P.M.
你可以過來吃晚餐嗎？下午五點如何？

talk
講話、談話、商討、表達思想

▷ Don't talk to your father like that.
不要像那樣和你父親說話。

▷ I'd like to talk to David.
我要和大衛說話。

▷ I want to talk to you.
我想和你談一談。

▷ I'd like to talk about my career.
我想要談一談我的事業。

▷ What did you talk to her?
你告訴她什麼事？

▷ I need to talk with you.
我需要和你談一談。

▷ We're talking about my career.
我們正在談我的事業。

▷ I don't know what you are talking about.
我不知道你在說什麼。

▷ Talk to me, honey.
親愛的，和我說話啊！(不要不理我)

▷ What are you talking about?
你在說什麼？

▷ We just talked about your marriage.
我們剛剛才談到關於你的婚姻的事。

▷ I'll talk to you later.
再見！

▷ Don't do it. You know how people talk.
不要這麼做。你是知道其他人會怎麼說的。

▷ It's time to talk business now.
現在該是談一談生意的時候了。

listen
留神聽、聽見、聽從

▷ I'm listening to the radio.
我在聽廣播。

▷ I enjoy listening to music.
我喜歡聽音樂。

▷ Listen, can you hear that?
聽好,你有聽見嗎?

▷ Listen to me, you should take a break.
聽我說,你應該休息一下。

▷ You should listen to your parents.
你應該聽你父母親的話。

▷ You are not listening to me.
你沒在聽我說。

▷ I warned him but he wouldn't listen.
我警告過他了,但是他不聽。

▷ You can listen to BBC radio online.
你可以在線上收聽 BBC 廣播。

相關用法

hear
聽見、無意間聽見

▷ I heard a funny noise.
我有聽到怪聲。

▷ I heard nothing.
我什麼都沒有聽見。

see

看見、知道、瞭解

▷ I see it!
我有看見。

▷ I saw nothing.
我沒有看見。

▷ I'm not seeing anything.
我沒有看見任何事情。

▷ I'm going to see a doctor.
我要去看醫生。

▷ Did you see that?
你有看見那個嗎？

▷ What did you see?
你看見了什麼？

▷ It was so dark I could hardly see.
真是暗，所以我不太能看見，

▷ Let me see your passport, please.
請給我看你的護照。

▷ Can you see what's going on over there?
你能看見那裡發生什麼事嗎？

▷ Can you see where I put my book?
你有看見我把書放在哪裡嗎？

▷ I saw him leaving the house.
我有看見他離開房子。

▷ I saw David murdered by John.
我有看見大衛被約翰謀殺了。

▷ I'm glad to see that you enjoy your work.
我很高興知道你喜歡你的工作。

▷ Do you see what I mean?
你瞭解我的意思嗎？

watch
注視、留意、當心

▷ I wasn't watching very closely.
我沒有看得非常仔細。

▷ Did you watch television tonight?
你今天晚上有看電視了嗎？

▷ Do you watch a lot of television?
你有看很多電視嗎？

▷ Watch me, honey.
親愛的，看著我。

▷ Watch how I do it.
看看我怎麼做的。

▷ You'd better watch David.
你最好要小心大衛。

▷ I'm watching television now.
我現在正在看電視。

▷ Watch out.
小心！

相關用法

look
看、注意、留神、看起來、期待

▷ What are you looking at?
你在看什麼？

▷ She looks happy.
她看上去很幸福。

▷ You look upset.
你看起來很沮喪！

know

知道、認出、精通(語言)、認識(某人)

▷ I don't know.
我不知道。

▷ I don't know for sure.
我不確定。

▷ I wouldn't know.
我不會知道。

▷ As far as I know he's abroad.
就我知道他人在國外。

▷ She said she didn't know.
她說過她不知道。

▷ Everyone knows that.
每個人都知道。

▷ I know that he didn't like it.
我知道他不喜歡。

▷ I know what I'm doing.
我知道我在做什麼。

▷ Do you know where David is?
你知道大衛在哪裡嗎？

▷ I know the answer to the question.
我知道問題的答案。

▷ What do you know about this accident?
你知道有關這件意外的什麼事嗎？

▷ I don't know anything about her.
我對她一無所知。

▷ Do you know French?
你懂法文嗎？

▷ I've known David for years.
我已經認識大衛很多年了。

read

閱讀、朗讀、察覺、攻讀

▷ I'm reading a book.
我正在看書。

▷ I like to read the romantic novels.
我喜歡看愛情小說。

▷ What are you reading?
你在讀什麼？

▷ I read a good article in today's paper.
我在今天的報紙上讀到了一篇好文章。

▷ I read about a murder in the newspaper.
我在報上看到了一件有關兇殺案件(的新聞)。

▷ Did you read the instructions before you operate it?
在操作之前你有詳閱說明書嗎？

▷ Did you read newspaper this morning?
你今天早上有看報嗎？

▷ I can read French but I can't speak it.
我可以看得懂法文，但我不會說。

▷ The little boy can read quite well now.
這個小男孩現在的閱讀能力很好。

▷ She read a story to the children.
她念故事給孩子們聽。

▷ She read his thoughts.
她看出了他的心思。

▷ John is reading law.
約翰在攻讀法律。

▷ David is reading history at Oxford.
大衛在牛津攻讀歷史。

study
學習、研究、細看

▷ He studies French.
他在學習法文。

▷ I studied hard.
我有用功讀書。

▷ He is studying to be a doctor.
他正在苦讀要成為一位醫生。

▷ I studied him closely.
我仔細地看了看他。

▷ She studied the report.
她研究了這個報告。

▷ For a year he studied Chinese with me.
他跟我學了一年中文。

▷ I studied him closely.
我仔細地看了看他。

▷ I often studies late into the night.
我常常讀書到深夜。

▷ He is studying geology in his room.
他正在他的房間裡念地質學。

▷ Next term we shall study how they grow.
下學期我們要學習他們如何成長的。

▷ He's been studying for his doctorate for 3 years already.
他已經念了三年的博士學位。

learn
學習、學會、獲悉

▷ The child is learning quickly.
這個小孩學習力很強。

▷ David is learning English now.
大衛現在正在學英語。

▷ I'm learning how to play the drums.
我正在學習怎麼打鼓。

▷ I'm trying to learn French.
我正試著學習法文。

▷ He has learnt a new skill.
他學會了一項新技能。

▷ You must learn that you can't do it.
你要知道，你不能這麼做。

▷ Where did you learn this news?
你從哪裡獲悉這則消息的？

▷ We learned the news this morning.
我們今天早晨獲悉這一則消息。

▷ They learn Russian at school.
他們在學校學的俄語。

▷ "Can you drive?" "I'm learning."
「你會開車嗎？」「我正在學。」

▷ I'm learning to play the piano.
我正在學彈鋼琴。

teach
教授、訓練、指導

▷ He teaches us English.
他教我們英文。

▷ He teaches in Seattle.
他在西雅圖教書。

▷ He teaches chemistry at the local junior school.
他在當地的中學教授化學課。

▷ Will you teach me?
你會教我嗎？

▷ My mother taught me this song.
我的母親教過我這首歌。

▷ My father taught me it when I was 12.
我的父親在我十二歲的時候教我的。

▷ I taught David how to write it.
我教大衛如何寫。

▷ I'll teach you to swim.
我會教你游泳。

▷ Who taught you to play the piano?
誰教你彈鋼琴的？

▷ Would you teach me how to use it?
你可以教我怎麼使用嗎？

buy
購買、獲得、相信、接受

▷ I'll buy it.
我要買。

▷ I'll buy this one.
我要買這一個。

▷ I'll buy a watch.
我要買一支錶。

▷ What are you going to buy?
你要買什麼？

▷ What did you buy?
你買了什麼？

▷ My father bought me a dog.
我父親買了一條狗給我。

▷ Mother bought me a pair of jeans.
母親給我買了一條牛仔褲。

▷ I'll buy you a present.
我會買禮物給你。

▷ Did you buy some apples?
你有買一些蘋果了嗎？

▷ If you say it's true, I'll buy it.
如果你說是真的，我會接受。

▷ I bought the house for $355000 in 2004.
我在 2004 年花三十五萬五千元買了這間房子。

▷ Let me buy you a drink.
我請你喝一杯。

sell
銷售、推銷、背叛、欺騙

▷ He sold me his camera.
他把他的照相機賣給我。

▷ He sold his bike to me for $10.
他以十美元的價錢把他的自行車賣給我。

▷ Do you sell stamps?
你們有賣郵票嗎？

▷ Do you sell cigarettes in this shop?
你們店裡有賣香菸嗎？

▷ Would you sell these apples to me?
你要賣這些蘋果給我嗎？

▷ I sold him the painting.
我賣給了他這幅畫。

▷ I'm thinking of selling my car.
我想要賣掉我的車了。

▷ I'll buy your house if you're willing to sell.
如果你願意賣，我要買你的房子。

▷ Television sells many products.
電視促進許多商品的銷售。

▷ We've been sold out.
我們被出賣了。

save
拯救、儲蓄、節省

▷ I'll save him.
我會救他。

▷ He saved me from drowning.
他救了我,讓我免於溺斃。

▷ You saved my life.
你救了我的命。

▷ The doctor saved the child's life.
這位醫生挽救了孩子的生命。

▷ They save their marriage by having another baby.
他們藉由再生一個孩子來拯救他們的婚姻。

▷ He promised to save a room for me.
他答應給我留個房間。

▷ You should learn to save.
你要學習存款。

▷ We're saving up for a new car.
我們正在存錢買車。

▷ Save it.
省省吧!(不必煩勞你)

▷ It will save you $100.
(你)將會省下一百元。

▷ If there is any food left over, save it for later.
如果有食物吃不完的,留著晚一點的時候再吃。

walk
走路、走過、散步、蹓(狗等)

▷ Walk, don't run.
用走的，不要跑。

▷ I like walking.
我喜歡步行。

▷ I walk to work.
我走路去上班。

▷ I just walked away.
我僅僅是走開。

▷ We have walked 2 miles today.
我們今天走了兩公里。

▷ He arose and walked to the window.
他站起來走向窗戶。

▷ Should I walk or call a taxi?
我應該用走的或是要搭計程車？

▷ I'll walk you home.
我送你回家。

▷ Do not walk to your car alone if you can avoid it.
盡量避免一個人走去開車。

▷ He's walking his dog.
他正在蹓他的狗。

▷ Can you walk my dog?
可以幫我蹓我的狗嗎？

▷ She walked the child out of the room.
她帶著孩子走出了房間。

sit
坐著、座落於、擺姿勢坐著、使就坐、合身

▷ He sat at his desk working.
他坐在位子上辦公。

▷ We're all sitting round the fire.
我們圍著爐火坐。

▷ They sat in a ring.
他們坐成一圈。

▷ I usually sat at the back of the class.
我通常坐在班上的最後面。

▷ Don't just sit there watching.
不要只是坐在那裡看。

▷ Sit down, please.
請坐。

▷ Come and sit over here.
過來坐在這裡。

▷ He sat beside me.
他坐在我旁邊。

▷ Where would you like to sit?
你(們)要坐在哪裡？

▷ We're sitting on opposite sides of a table.
我們隔著桌子坐在對面。

▷ She sat the child in the chair.
她把孩子放在椅子上。

▷ The temple sits on a hill.
寺廟座落在山上。

▷ He sat for his portrait.
他坐著讓人給他畫像。

▷ The suit sits well on him.
那套西裝他穿很合身。

stand

站立、站著、站起、處於某種狀態

▷ He stood there thinking about that.
他站著思考那件事。

▷ She stands up.
她站起來。

▷ I stood up and I said, hey!
我站起來說嗨。

▷ He stood up to read the lesson.
他站起來念課文。

▷ He stood where he'd always stood.
他站在他老是站著的地方。

▷ Don't just stand there; help me.
不要只是站在哪裡，幫幫我。

▷ I had to stand.
我只好站著。

▷ Her legs were so weak that she could hardly stand.
她的腿虛弱得幾乎站不住了。

▷ Just stand where you are.
就站在你現在所處的地方。

▷ He stood the ladder against the wall.
他把梯子靠牆放著。

▷ He stands high in the public estimation.
他在公眾中聲望很高。

stay

停留、留下、繼續、保持、站住

▷ Stay right here.
就在這裡停下。

▷ I can't stay with you.
我不能留下來陪你。

▷ I stayed late at the party last night.
我昨天晚上在宴會上待到很晚。

▷ Can you stay for dinner?
你可以留下來吃晚餐嗎？

▷ Don't turn off here; stay on this road.
不要在這裡轉彎，留在這條路上。

▷ Stay away from her.
離她遠一點。

▷ I stayed up until 2 A.M.
我熬夜到早上兩點。

▷ Where are you going to stay?
你要住在哪裡？

▷ My mother is staying with us this week.
我媽媽這整個星期都留下來陪我們。

▷ She is going to stay in Seattle.
她要留在西雅圖。

▷ I stayed the night at a friend's house.
我在一個朋友家過夜。

▷ The weather has stayed warm all week.
這整個星期天氣都很溫暖。

▷ I hope the weather will stay fine.
我希望天氣能持續放晴。

sleep

睡、睡覺、可供(人)住宿、與⋯上床

▷ She is sleeping now.
她現在正在睡覺。

▷ He was still sleeping when I went in.
我走進去時他還在睡覺。

▷ I slept very badly last night.
咋天夜裡我睡得很不好。

▷ I didn't sleep very well.
我睡得不安穩。

▷ Did you sleep well last night?
你昨晚睡得好嗎？

▷ I usually sleep late on Sundays.
星期天我通常很晚起床。

▷ He likes to sleep for an hour in the afternoon.
他喜歡在中午小睡一個小時。

▷ She hoped to sleep off her headache.
她希望睡一覺後頭痛會痊癒。

▷ How many guests can the motel sleep?
這家汽車旅館可供多少客人住宿？

▷ Did you sleep with her?
你有和她上床嗎？

wake
醒來、起床、喚醒

▷ Wake up, David.
大衛，起床囉！

▷ Wake up, guys.
你們大家清醒一點吧！

▷ She usually wakes up early.
她通常很早起床。

▷ I woke up at six this morning.
今天早晨我六點醒來。

▷ He woke up late.
他很晚起床。

▷ When did you wake up?
你幾點起床的？

▷ Did you wake up?
你醒了嗎？

▷ I woke him up.
我叫醒了他。

▷ Please wake me up at 7:00.
請在七點的時候叫醒我。

▷ Please wake me early tomorrow.
明天請早一點叫我起床。

▷ I woke up with a headache.
我起床時頭很痛。

▷ Come on, wake up - breakfast is ready.
快一點起床，早餐好了。

▷ He woke himself up with his own snoring!
他被自己的鼾聲吵醒。

wash
洗、洗滌、洗掉、耐洗、洗刷(罪過)

▷ I washed my gloves.
我洗了我的手套。

▷ She washed her face, then went downstairs.
她洗了臉之後走下樓去。

▷ He likes to wash in cold water.
他喜歡用冷水洗澡。

▷ This cloth washes well.
這種布很耐洗。

▷ They washed those marks off the wall.
他們把牆上的那些印記洗掉了。

▷ He is trying to wash away his sins.
他正試圖洗刷他的罪過。

▷ This shirt needs washing.
這件襯衫需要清洗。

▷ She washed and then went to bed.
她簡單清洗後就上床睡覺了。

▷ Did you wash your hair?
你有洗頭髮嗎？

▷ I forgot to wash my hands.
我忘記洗手了。

feel

摸、觸、試探、感覺、感受、認為、以為

▷ I can't feel where the light switch is.
我摸不出電燈開關在哪裡。

▷ He felt the cloth to see its quality.
他摸摸布看它的品質。

▷ I felt the house shake.
我有感覺房子在震動。

▷ I felt an insect crawling up my leg.
我感到有一隻蟲子順著我的腿往上爬。

▷ I felt the wind blowing on my face from an open window.
我感到風從開著的窗戶吹到我的臉上。

▷ He felt no shame and no regret.
他不感到羞愧，也不感到遺憾。

▷ You won't feel the slightest pain.
你一點也不會感到痛的。

▷ I felt rather sick to my stomach.
我覺得我的胃不舒服。

▷ I feel stupid.
我覺得很呆。

▷ I felt that she was very weak.
我覺得她很虛弱。

▷ I felt myself unable to leave the city.
我覺得自己離不開這座城市了。

▷ My eyes feel really sore.
我的眼睛真的感覺好痛。

▷ How are you feeling?
你現在感覺如何？

touch

接觸、碰到、感動

▷ Don't touch.
不要碰！

▷ Did you touch it?
你有碰過嗎？

▷ Don't touch my daughter.
不要碰我女兒。

▷ Don't touch the exhibits.
不要碰展覽品。

▷ Don't touch anything until we arrive.
我們抵達之前不要碰任何東西。

▷ She lightly touched his forehead.
她輕輕地摸了摸他的前額。

▷ They sat so close that their heads nearly touched.
他們坐得那麼近，頭幾乎碰到一起了。

▷ I swore I'd never touch the drink.
我發誓我不會再碰酒。

▷ I was touched beyond words.
我感動莫名。

▷ That paint is wet - don't touch it.
那幅畫還沒乾，不要碰。

▷ No thanks, I never touch alcohol.
不了，謝謝，我從不碰酒。

▷ Honestly, I haven't touched a drop all night.
老實說，我整晚都沒有喝一滴酒。

wait
等、等待、已準備好、服侍、伺候

▷ Wait a moment.
等一下。

▷ Wait a second.
等一下。

▷ Wait for me.
等等我。

▷ What are you waiting for?
你在等什麼？

▷ I'm waiting for one of my friends.
我在等我的一個朋友。

▷ Did you wait for David?
你有等大衛嗎？

▷ I'm waiting to have a word with you.
我正等著和你說話。

▷ We're waiting for the bus.
我們正在等公車。

▷ They waited for David's arrival.
他們在等大衛的到來。

▷ Your dinner is waiting.
你的晚餐已經(做)好了。

▷ The old man has no one to wait on him.
那個老人沒有人服侍。

▷ He held her hand and waited the answer.
他握著她的手等待回答。

▷ Don't wait supper for me.
別等我吃晚飯。

arrive
到達、到來、達成、(嬰兒)出生

▷ I just arrived in Seattle yesterday.
我昨天才抵達西雅圖的。

▷ We arrived home safely.
我們安全地抵達家門。

▷ When did you arrive in Seattle?
你什麼時候抵達西雅圖的？

▷ What time does the plane arrive in Seattle?
飛機什麼時候抵達西雅圖？

▷ He arrived in London last Monday.
他上星期一抵達倫敦。

▷ When should I arrive at the airport?
我應該什麼時候抵達機場？

▷ We arrived at the airport at four.
我們四點到達了機場。

▷ The books will arrive tomorrow.
書明天就會到。

▷ Has the post arrived yet?
信件寄到了嗎？

▷ Her baby arrived yesterday.
她的孩子昨天出生了。

▷ What decision did you finally arrive at?
你們最後達成了什麼決定？

leave

離開、遺棄、辭去、留給、死後留下、剩下

▷ When are you going to leave?
你什麼時候要離開？

▷ He left his house at 2 P.M.
他下午兩點離開他的房子的。

▷ Mr. Smith left the room at two o'clock.
史密斯先生兩點離開房間的。

▷ We will leave for Seattle next week.
我們下週會動身去西雅圖。

▷ They left for New York.
他們已經去紐約了。

▷ Her husband has left her.
她的丈夫把她遺棄了。

▷ Maria left school last year and she is working in a shop now.
瑪莉亞去年退學了，現正在一家商店工作。

▷ I left my keys behind.
我忘了帶鑰匙。

▷ He left me a few books.
他留給我幾本書。

▷ You can leave your case with me.
你可以把箱子交給我。

▷ He left a wife and five children.
他死後留下妻子和五個孩子。

▷ Anything left?
有什麼剩下來嗎？

▷ I saw him leaving the house.
我有看見他離開房子。

open
打開、開始、開張營業、展開

▷ Did you open the door?
你有打開門嗎？

▷ Did you open the umbrella?
你有開傘嗎？

▷ Open the door for me.
幫我開門。

▷ Open your mouth.
打開你的嘴巴。

▷ Open your book.
打開你的書。

▷ How did you open the box?
你怎麼打開盒子的？

▷ I won't open the window.
我不會開窗戶的。

▷ I opened the window after I got up.
我起床後便把窗子打開。

▷ The Conference was opened on October 15.
大會於十月十五日開始。

▷ He opened a grocery store last month.
上個月他開了一間雜貨店。

▷ The shop opens at 9 A.M.
商店早上九點開始營業。

▷ The flowers are opening.
花正在開放。

▷ The fair opened on March 17.
交易會於三月十七日開幕。

close
關閉、關(商店等)、封閉(道路等)

▷ Close the window.
關上窗戶。

▷ Close your eyes and go to sleep.
閉上你的眼睛去睡覺。

▷ Did you close the gate last night?
你昨天晚上有關門嗎?

▷ Could you close the window for me?
可以幫我關上窗戶嗎?

▷ She closed the door.
她關上門了。

▷ The post office closes at 6 P.M.
郵局晚上六點關門。

▷ What time does the bank close?
銀行何時關門的?

▷ What time does the park close?
公園何時關閉的?

▷ I have closed my account at that bank.
我已經關了我在該銀行的帳戶。

▷ The firm has decided to close its Seattle branch.
公司已經決定結束它在西雅圖的分公司業務。

▷ We're forced to close the local hospital.
我們被迫關閉當地醫院。

▷ The conference was closed on June 10.
會議於六月十日結束。

〔附錄〕動詞三態

現在	過去	過去分詞
answer	answered	answered
arrive	arrived	arrived
buy	bought	bought
call	called	called
close	closed	closed
come	came	come
do	did	done
feel	felt	felt
get	got	gotten
give	gave	given
go	went	gone
have	had	had
hear	heard	heard
keep	kept	kept
know	knew	known
learn	learned	learned
leave	left	left
like	liked	liked
listen	listened	listened
look	looked	looked
make	made	made
need	needed	needed
open	opened	opened
read	read	read

現在	過去	過去分詞
save	saved	saved
say	said	said
see	saw	seen
sell	sold	sold
sit	sat	sat
sleep	slept	slept
stand	stood	stood
stay	stayed	stayed
study	studied	studied
take	took	taken
talk	talked	talked
teach	taught	taught
tell	told	told
think	thought	thought
touch	touched	touched
try	tried	tried
turn	turned	turned
wait	waited	waited
wake	woke	woken
walk	walked	walked
want	wanted	wanted
wash	washed	washed
watch	watched	watched

Part

3

好用動詞片語

agree with
同意某人(的看法)

▷ I agree with you.
我同意你(的看法)。

▷ We agree with you.
我們同意你(的看法)。

▷ He agreed with me.
他同意了我(的看法)。

▷ I agree with David on this point.
在這一點上我同意大衛(的看法)。

▷ I don't agree with you.
我不同意你(的看法)。

▷ I don't agree with you on this.
在這件事上，我不同意你。

▷ I can't agree with him on this matter.
這個問題上我不同意他的意見。

▷ He agreed with me that we should leave.
他同意我的看法，認為我們應該要離開。

▷ Do you agree with me?
你同意我(的看法)嗎？

▷ Why don't you agree with him?
為什麼你不同意他(的看法)？

▷ I know why you didn't agree with her.
我知道你為什麼不同意她(的看法)。

▷ I couldn't agree with you more.
我非常同意你(的看法)。

▷ I couldn't agree with you less.
我非常不同意你(的看法)。

▷ Yes, I do agree with you.
是的，我的確同意你(的看法)。

agree to

同意(某事)

▷ Do you agree to it?
你同意(這件事)嗎?

▷ Do you agree to my plan?
你同意我的計畫嗎?

▷ I agree to it.
我同意(這件事)。

▷ I agree to your advice.
我同意你的建議。

▷ I agree to do it.
我同意去做這件事。

▷ I agree to finish this project.
我同意去完成這個計畫案。

▷ I agree to write it down.
我同意寫下來。

▷ I agree to go with you.
我同意和你去。

▷ David agreed to help Maria.
大衛同意幫助瑪莉亞了。

▷ He agrees to your proposal.
他同意你的計畫。

▷ I agree to your comment.
我同意你的評論。

▷ I agree to your point on this project.
我同意你在這個企畫案的觀點。

▷ I agree to his idea that we go at once.
我同意他認為我們立刻去的想法。

▷ Don't you agree to it?
你不同意嗎?

pick up
撿起、搭載、學會

▷ Did you pick it up?
你有撿起來嗎?

▷ Will you pick it up?
你會撿起來嗎?

▷ Please pick it up for me.
請幫我撿起來。

▷ I just picked up the hat.
我剛剛撿起了帽子。

▷ Pick up the book, please.
請撿起書本。

▷ Did you pick your sister up?
你有去接你的姊妹嗎?

▷ I'll pick you up.
我會去接你。

▷ I'll pick you up at ten o'clock.
我會在十點去接你。

▷ I'll pick you up tomorrow.
我明天會去接你。

▷ I'd love to pick you up.
我很樂意去接你。

▷ Let him pick you up.
讓他去接你。

▷ He wants me to pick him up.
他希望我去接他。

▷ I can't pick her up so many times.
我無法去接她這麼多次。

▷ Where did you pick up your English?
你在哪裡學的英文?

put on
穿上、戴上(強調「穿」的動作)

▷ Put on your glasses.
戴上你的眼鏡。

▷ Put on your coat.
穿上你的外套。

▷ Why don't you put on your pants?
為什麼你不穿上你的褲子？

▷ If you feel cold, put on your gloves.
如果你覺得冷，就戴上你的手套。

▷ I want to put my scarf on.
我想要戴上我的圍巾。

▷ Help her put it on.
幫她穿上。

▷ Did you ask David to put it on?
你有叫大衛穿上嗎？

▷ David put on his uniform.
大衛穿上了他的制服。

相關用法

take off
脫下(強調「脫」的動作)、起飛

▷ Take your coat off and sit down.
脫掉外套坐下吧！

▷ Let me take it off for you.
讓我幫你脫下。

▷ The plane had already taken off.
飛機已經起飛了。

call at
拜訪(某地)

▷ I called at many places.
我去過許多地方。

▷ I called at my aunt's.
我去我姑姑家拜訪。

▷ I called at his mother's place.
我去他母親的家裡拜訪。

▷ I called at an old friend's.
我去了一位老朋友家。

▷ I called at her home.
我去了她家。

▷ I called at the Smith's yesterday.
我昨天去了史密斯家。

▷ I'll call at the Smith's house tomorrow.
明天我將去史密斯家拜訪。

▷ I called at our new neighbor's house.
我去了我們新鄰居家拜訪。

▷ I'll call at your office tomorrow.
我明天會去你的辦公室拜訪。

▷ I'll call at your address tonight.
我今晚會去你家拜訪。

▷ I called at the doctor's yesterday.
我昨天去了醫務室。

▷ I called at the post office.
我去了郵局。

▷ I called at Mr. Penny's office.
我去了潘尼先生的辦公室。

▷ On the way back, we called at Hawaii.
回程的路上，我們去了趟夏威夷。

call on/upon
拜訪(某人)、號召

▷ I'll call on you.
我會去找你。

▷ I'll call on you later.
晚一點我會去找你。

▷ I'll call on you later today.
今天晚一點我會去找你。

▷ I'll call on you next week.
我下星期會去看你。

▷ I'll call on you sometime next week.
下星期我會找個時間去找你。

▷ I'll call on you tomorrow around noon.
明天大概中午的時候，我會去找你。

▷ I'll call on you some other day.
改天我會去找你。

▷ I'll call on him on my way home.
回家的路上，我會去找他。

▷ I'll call on David when I get to Seattle.
當我到西雅圖的時候，我會去找大衛。

▷ They'll call on us very soon.
他們很快就會來拜訪我們。

▷ I called on the doctor yesterday.
我昨天去拜訪了醫生。

▷ I called on the Smiths yesterday.
我昨天拜訪了史密斯一家人。

▷ She called on me to make a speech.
她有要求我發表演說。

call off
取消、叫開、把(思想)轉移開

▷ The game will be called off.
比賽將會被取消。

▷ The concert was called off.
音樂會被取消了。

▷ Our wedding was called off.
我們的婚禮被取消了。

▷ The strike was called off again.
罷工又被取消了。

▷ The football match was called off.
足球賽被取消了。

▷ It was called off at the very last minute.
在最後一刻被取消了。

▷ Why was the football match called off?
為什麼取消足球賽？

▷ Will you call off the meeting?
你會取消會議嗎？

▷ When was the meeting called off?
會議什麼時候被取消的？

▷ I didn't know the game was called off.
我不知道比賽被取消了。

▷ The meeting has been called off.
會議已經被取消了。

▷ Call off your dog, will you?
把你的狗叫開好嗎？

▷ However, the event was called off.
總之，活動被取消了。

call up

給…打電話、喚醒、憶起

▷ I'll call you up tomorrow.
我明天會打電話給你。

▷ I'll call you up this evening.
今天晚上我會打電話給你。

▷ I'll call David up every Saturday night.
每個星期六晚上我都會打電話給大衛。

▷ She may call you up tonight.
今晚她可能會打電話給你。

▷ When I call you up and you're not there.
我打電話給你的時候，你不在。

▷ Call him up and tell him what you want.
打電話給他，告訴他你的想法。

▷ Don't call him up anymore.
不要再打電話給他。

▷ Could you call him up?
你可以打電話給他嗎？

▷ Just call her up to say you're sorry.
只要打電話給她道歉就可以了。

▷ Please call me up at six A.M.
請明天早上六點叫醒我。

▷ This photo called up memories of our last trip.
這張照片使我們想起了上次的旅行。

▷ Your letter called up the days when we worked together.
你的信使我們回想起一同工作的日子。

care about
對…感興趣、關心、擔心、注意

▷ I care about you.
我關心你。

▷ I care about your marriage.
我關心你的婚姻。

▷ I only care about you.
我只在乎你。

▷ I really care about you.
我真的很關心你。

▷ I do care about David.
我確實很關心大衛。

▷ I don't care about your opinion.
我對你的觀點不感興趣。

▷ You care about nothing.
你什麼都不在意。

▷ You should care about your sister.
你應該關心一下你的姊妹。

▷ She doesn't care about other people.
她只顧她自己。

▷ What do you care about?
你在意什麼？

▷ What topics do you care about?
你關心什麼議題？

▷ Do you care about my studies?
你有關心我的功課嗎？

▷ Do you care about the Oscars?
你有關心奧斯卡？

▷ Don't you care about losing your job?
難道你不擔心失去工作嗎？

check in
在旅館登記住宿、報到

▷ Check in, please.
麻煩你(我要)辦理報到。

▷ Can I check in now?
我現在可以辦理報到嗎?

▷ Can I check in here?
我可以在這裡辦理報到嗎?

▷ I'd like to check in.
我要辦理報到。

▷ We have just checked in at the hotel.
我們剛剛在旅館辦好住宿手續。

▷ Where may I check in for CA Airlines?
我要到哪裡辦理 CA 航空登機手續?

▷ Where may I check in?
我該在哪裡辦理登機手續?

▷ Do you have any baggage to check in?
你有行李要托運嗎?

相關用法

check out
結帳、借出

▷ Check out, please.
麻煩你(我要)結帳。

▷ Can I check out now?
我現在可以辦理結帳嗎?

▷ We'd like to check out, please.
麻煩你,我們要辦理結帳。

clean up
清理乾淨、梳洗、根除(社會弊端等)

▷ Just clean it up now.
現在就清理乾淨。

▷ Clean up the pieces of broken bottle.
把瓶子的碎片清理乾淨。

▷ I'll clean up my room later.
我等一下會清理我的房間。

▷ I cleaned up my room yesterday.
我昨天有清理我的房間了。

▷ I've cleaned up my room last week.
我上星期已經有清理我的房間了。

▷ She's cleaning up the kitchen now.
她現在正在打掃廚房。

▷ David is cleaning up the mess.
大衛正在打掃這堆亂七八糟的東西。

▷ You have to clean it up.
你應該要清理乾淨。

▷ Did you clean up your table yesterday?
你昨天有清理乾淨你的桌子嗎？

▷ Does Maria clean up her room?
瑪莉亞有清理乾淨她的房間嗎？

▷ Would you clean it up right now?
你可以現在就清理乾淨嗎？

▷ Wait a minute. I'll have to clean up.
等一下。我要梳洗一下。

▷ The mayor has decided to clean up the city.
市長已下決心要整頓市容。

dedicate...to

獻身於、獻給…、題獻(著作)

▷ David dedicated his life to church.
　大衛把一生獻給了教堂。

▷ He dedicated his life to science.
　他把他的一生獻給了科學。

▷ He dedicated his life to Taiwan.
　他把他的一生獻給了台灣。

▷ He dedicated his whole life to music.
　他把他畢生的精力獻給了音樂。

▷ David dedicated his life to his country.
　大衛把畢生的精力獻給了他的國家。

▷ He dedicated himself to his studies.
　他一生致力於他的學術。

▷ He dedicated his life to changing it.
　他一生致力於改變它。

▷ He dedicated himself to finding a cure.
　他將自己奉獻於找出醫治的方法。

▷ He totally dedicated himself to making this film.
　他把畢生的精力致力於拍這部電影。

▷ He dedicated himself to making that dream a reality.
　他把畢生的精力致力實現夢想。

▷ The writer dedicated his first book to his mother.
　作者把他的第一本書獻給他的母親。

depend on
取決於、依靠

▷ It depends on.
看情況！

▷ It depends on the weather.
視天氣狀況而定。

▷ It depends on the circumstances.
視環境狀況而定。

▷ It depends on your decision.
視你的決定而定。

▷ It depends on your son.
視你的兒子的狀況而定。

▷ It will depend on your plans.
視你的計畫而定。

▷ It depends on the meaning of marriage.
視婚姻的定義而定。

▷ It depends on what you pay.
視你的付出而定。

▷ It depends on what you meant.
視你的看法而定。

▷ It depends on where you choose.
視你的選擇而定。

▷ It depends on what you're saying.
視你的發言而定。

▷ His success depends on himself.
他的成功靠他自己。

▷ It'll depend on the weather.
將視天氣而定。

▷ You can depend on him.
你可以信賴他。

find out

發現、查出、找出

▷ What did you find out?
你發現了什麼？

▷ What did you try to find out?
你試圖查出了什麼？

▷ I tried to find out his plans.
我試圖要查出他的計畫。

▷ David tried to find out the truth.
大衛試圖要查出真相。

▷ We tried to find out the whole story.
我們試圖將整件事查個水落石出。

▷ They are trying to find out his secrets.
他們正試圖找出他的秘密。

▷ Did you find out anything?
你有發現任何事了嗎？

▷ Did you find out why he was absent from class?
你弄清楚他缺課的原因了嗎？

相關用法

check out

檢查

▷ I'll check it out.
我會查出來的。

▷ Let me check it out right now.
我現在就馬上查一下。

be/get used to

習慣於

▷ I'm used to hard work.
我習慣於辛苦的工作。

▷ He's not used to New York.
他不習慣紐約。

▷ He's not used to western food.
他不習慣(吃)西餐。

▷ Are you used to fast food?
你習慣速食嗎？

▷ We're used to his strange behavior.
我們習慣於他怪異的行為。

▷ I'm used to working late.
我習慣於工作到很晚。

▷ I'm used to working hard.
我習慣於努力工作。

▷ We are used to working together.
我們習慣於一起工作。

▷ Are you used to cooking?
你習慣下廚嗎？

▷ I'm used to driving on the left.
我習慣開車靠左邊。

▷ I'm not used to wearing glasses.
我不習慣戴眼鏡。

▷ Maria is used to taking bus.
瑪莉亞習慣搭公車。

▷ He is not used to living in New York.
他不習慣住在紐約。

▷ David is used to listening to pop music.
大衛習慣聽流行音樂。

get on
上車(火車等)、騎上(機車)、穿、變老、過日子

▷ Hurry up. Get on!
快點！上車吧！

▷ When did you get on the bus?
你什麼時候搭上公車的？

▷ Get on my bike.
騎上我的腳踏車吧！

▷ How are you getting on recently?
你近來過得怎樣？

▷ Everything was getting on very well.
一切都進行得很順利了。

▷ You should get your jacket on.
你應該要穿上外套。

▷ It is getting on midnight.
快要半夜了。

▷ How do I get on yahoo?
我要如何登入 yahoo？

相關用法

get off
下車、離開、出發、弄走、弄掉

▷ How do I get off yahoo?
我要如何登出 yahoo？

▷ I need to get off the bus at the next stop.
我要在下一站下車。

▷ It's dangerous to sit on the roof. Get off!
坐在屋頂很危險。下來！

get rid of
擺脫、消除

▷ I need to get rid of them.
我需要擺脫他們。

▷ He can't get rid of the cold.
他的感冒老是好不了。

▷ You should get rid of smoking.
你應該戒煙。

▷ My grandpa says we should get rid of it.
我爺爺說，我們應該要擺脫它。

▷ It is hard to get rid of a bad habit.
壞習慣很難戒除。

▷ How to get rid of my headache?
要如何擺脫我的頭痛？

▷ How to get rid of unwanted suitors?
要如何擺脫不請自來的求婚者？

▷ How do I get rid of all this cocaine?
我要如何擺脫古柯鹼？

▷ How do I get rid of that horrible smell?
我要如何清除異味？

▷ How should I get rid of dark circles under my eyes?
我要如何清除我眼睛的黑眼圈？

▷ How should I get rid of this feeling?
我要如何擺脫這個感覺？

▷ Please help me get rid of the paint smell.
請幫我清除油漆的味道。

get through

度過難關、通過(考試)、完成、接通電話

▷ You'll get through it.
你會辦得到的。

▷ You're going to get through this.
你將會完成這件事的。

▷ How can we get through this?
我們要如何度過這個難關呢？

▷ How did you get through it?
你是如何熬過來的？

▷ How do I get through without you?
沒有你我該如何能熬過？

▷ I can't believe you got through it.
我真是不敢相信你熬過來了。

▷ We will get through this hard time.
我們會度過難關的。

▷ How can I get through the Holidays?
我要如何熬過這些節日？

▷ He got through his task as quickly as possible.
他盡快地完成了他的工作。

▷ I called you but didn't get through.
我有打電話給你了，但是沒有接通。

▷ I made a phone call but didn't get through.
我有打電話了，但是沒有接通。

get together
相聚

▷ Let's get together sometime.
我們找個時間聚聚。

▷ Let's get together sometime this summer.
今年夏天我們找個時間聚聚。

▷ We always get together during summer vacation.
暑假期間我們都會聚會。

▷ We get together once a year at Christmas.
我們每年耶誕節聚會一次。

▷ Anybody wants to get together?
有誰想要聚會嗎?

▷ When can we get together?
我們何時可以聚會?

▷ When do you want to get together?
你(們)要什麼時候聚會?

▷ Where do you want to get together?
你(們)要在哪裡聚會?

▷ What time do you want to get together next time?
下一次你(們)要什麼時候聚會?

▷ Do you want to get together for coffee?
你(們)要喝杯咖啡見個面嗎?

▷ Do you want to get together again.
你(們)要再聚會嗎?

get up
(使)起床、站起來、籌備、變得猛烈

▷ I got up early.
我很早就起床了。

▷ Today I got up carly.
今天我很早就起床了。

▷ I got up late.
我很晚才起床。

▷ I get up at 7 A.M. every day.
我每天早上十點起床。

▷ I usually get up at six A.M.
我通常早上六點起床。

▷ When did you get up?
你什麼時候起床的?

▷ I checked my e-mail when I got up on Sunday morning.
我星期天早上起床時,都會收我的電子郵件。

▷ Since he got up late, he missed the bus.
因為他晚起床,所以錯過公車。

▷ What time did you get up this morning?
你今天早上幾點起床?

▷ When do you usually get up?
你通常什麼時間起床?

▷ Did you get up on time?
你有準時起床嗎?

▷ We are getting up a play for next week.
我們正在安排下星期的演出。

▷ The wind is getting up.
風越刮越大。

give up
放棄、停止(做某事)、讓出

▷ I gave up.
我放棄了。

▷ I won't give up.
我不會放棄。

▷ You will give up, won't you?
你會放棄吧，對嗎？

▷ We gave up a while ago.
我們放棄好一陣子了。

▷ We gave up a lot when we left.
我們離開時，我們就完全放棄了。

▷ Don't give up.
不要放棄。

▷ Why did you give up?
你為什麼要放棄？

▷ Why don't you just give up?
你為什麼不乾脆放棄？

▷ The reason why I gave up is you.
我放棄的理由是因為你。

▷ She gave up her children to her ex-husband.
她將她的孩子給了她的前夫。

▷ He asked me to give up smoking.
他要我戒煙。

▷ I wish I could give up drinking.
我真希望自己能戒酒。

▷ He gave up his seat to an elder man.
他讓座給一位老人。

hang up
掛上電話、推遲

▷ Don't hang up.
不要掛斷(電話)。

▷ Don't hang up on the telephone
不要掛斷電話。

▷ I said goodbye and hung up.
我說再見然後就掛斷(電話)了。

▷ I just hung up the phone on my dad.
我掛斷了我父親的電話。

▷ Someone hung up the phone on me.
有人掛斷我的電話。

▷ I just hung up the phone without saying goodbye.
我沒有說再見就掛斷電話了。

▷ She hung up on me.
她不等我說完便掛斷電話了。

▷ David hung up the phone immediately.
大衛立即就掛斷電話了。

▷ Who hang up my cellular phone?
誰掛我的手機？

▷ She was very angry and hung up the phone.
她很生氣並掛斷了電話。

▷ When did you hang up the phone?
你什麼時候掛斷電話的？

▷ The peace talks were hung up.
和談中斷了。

▷ The project was hung up for lack of fund.
工程由於缺少資金而被擱置。

hang on

握住不放、堅持下去、(打電話時)不掛斷

▷ Hang on.
　堅持下去。

▷ Hang on, OK?
　堅持下去，好嗎？

▷ Hang on, honey.
　親愛的，要堅持下去。

▷ He hung on until the rope broke.
　他抓緊著直到繩子斷了。

▷ Try to hang on.
　要設法堅持下去。

▷ Hang on, please.
　請等一下。

▷ Hang on a second.
　不要掛斷(電話)。

▷ Try to hang on a bit longer.
　再等一下不要掛斷電話。

▷ Hang on for a moment, please.
　請再等一下不要掛斷電話。

▷ Would you please hang on?
　可以請您等一下不要掛斷電話嗎？

▷ Hang on! I'll be back in a minute.
　等一下。我馬上回來。

▷ The line is busy, would you like to hang on?
　電話佔線中，請別掛斷好嗎？

hang out
閒逛、打發時間

▷ I used to hang out in this place.
我以前習慣在這裡閒逛。

▷ I like to hang out with David.
我喜歡和大衛在一起。

▷ I like to hang out at my best friend's house.
我喜歡去我最好的朋友家打發時間。

▷ I love to hang out in the woods outside my home.
我喜歡去我家外面的森林裡閒逛。

▷ He hangs out in Green Street.
他去綠街閒逛。

▷ We always hang out in the pub.
我們總在酒吧裡打發時間。

▷ We spend a lot of time just hanging out.
我們老是在一起打發時間。

▷ David and I hang out a lot.
大衛和我老是廝混在一起。

▷ Would you like to hang out like old times?
你要像我們以前一樣到處逛逛嗎？

▷ Do you wanna hang out with me tonight?
今晚你要和我出去逛逛嗎？

laugh at
嘲笑、因…發笑

▷ I wouldn't laugh at you.
我不會嘲笑你。

▷ They always laugh at me.
他們總是嘲笑我。

▷ I laugh at his comments.
我嘲笑他的評論。

▷ His friends laugh at David.
他的朋友們嘲笑大衛。

▷ We laugh at his eating habits.
我們嘲笑他的飲食習慣。

▷ You shouldn't laugh at your brother.
你不應該嘲笑你的兄弟。

▷ They laugh at him.
他們嘲笑他。

▷ Don't laugh at me.
不要嘲笑我。

▷ Don't laugh at people in trouble.
不要幸災樂禍。

▷ Are you laughing at me?
你在嘲笑我嗎？

▷ Why did you laugh at me?
你為什麼要嘲笑我？

▷ What are you laughing at?
你在嘲笑什麼？

▷ I always laugh at his jokes.
我總是因為他的笑話大笑。

take back
收回(所說的話)、拿回

▷ Take it back.
收回去。

▷ I take back what I said.
我收回我說過的話。

▷ I can't take it back.
我無法收回。

▷ I've decided to take back my book.
我已經決定要拿回我的書。

▷ She finally took back her words.
她最終收回了她的話。

▷ David already took it back.
大衛已經取回了。

▷ You'll take it back, won't you?
你會收回，對嗎？

▷ He won't take it back!
他不會收回的。

▷ Let me take back my money.
我要收回我的錢。

▷ Please take it back for me.
請為我收回。

▷ Please take back my computer.
請拿回我的電腦。

▷ Why don't you just take it back?
你為什麼不乾脆收回？

▷ They won't take it back because of some
reasons.
因為某些原因，他們不會收回。

take care of
照顧、照料

▷ Take care of yourself.
照顧好自己。

▷ Take care of the baby while I am out.
我出去時，(請你)照顧一下孩子。

▷ Would you take care of it?
可以請你照顧一下嗎？

▷ Please take care of my parents.
請照顧我的父母。

▷ Do you know how to take care of it?
你知道要如何照顧它嗎？

▷ How should I take care of my piano?
我要如何維護我的鋼琴？

▷ How can I take care of my feet?
我要如何照護我的腳？

▷ What's the best way to take care of my Christmas tree?
照顧我的耶誕樹最好的方法為何？

相關用法

look after
照顧

▷ Would you look after my dog?
可以照顧一下我的狗嗎？

▷ Who's going to look after my children?
誰要照料我的孩子們？

wake up
喚醒、覺醒、振作

▷ Wake up, honey.
親愛的，醒醒！

▷ Wake up, David.
大衛的，醒醒！

▷ Wake me up at five A.M.
早上五點叫醒我！

▷ Come on, wake up.
好了，醒醒吧！

▷ I woke up at seven o'clock.
我七點就起床了。

▷ When did you wake up?
你什麼時候醒來的？

▷ When did you wake him up?
你什麼時候叫醒他的？

▷ How did you wake up today?
你今天怎麼醒來的？

▷ What time did you wake up this morning?
你今天早上幾點醒來的？

▷ Did you wake her up at six o'clock?
你有在六點的時候叫醒她嗎？

▷ Did you wake up because of noises?
你因為噪音才醒來的嗎？

▷ We always wake up at seven A.M.
我們總是在早上七點醒來。

▷ I usually wake up at six in the morning.
我通常在早上六點醒來。

▷ This event may wake him up.
這件事也許能使他覺悟。

write down
寫下、記錄

▷ Did you write it down?
你有寫下來了嗎？

▷ Will you write it down?
你會記錄下來嗎？

▷ Please write it down.
請記錄下來。

▷ Write it down for me.
請幫我記錄下來。

▷ Write down your name.
寫下你的名字。

▷ Write down your passwords.
寫下你的密碼。

▷ Write down your thoughts.
寫下你的想法。

▷ What did you write down?
你記錄了什麼？

▷ Will you write down your address?
你會寫下你的地址嗎？

▷ Can you write down this, if possible?
如果可能的話，可以寫下這個嗎？

▷ Write down your name on the back of the photos.
在相片的背面寫下你的名字。

turn on

打開(電燈、瓦斯、音響等)的開關

▷ Turn it on, please.
　請打開。

▷ I didn't turn it on.
　我沒有打開。

▷ Will you turn it on?
　你會打開嗎？

▷ I turned on the radio.
　我打開了收音機。

▷ Did you turn on the TV?
　你有打開電視了嗎？

▷ Did you turn on the lights?
　你有打開電燈了嗎？

▷ When did you turn on the heat?
　你什麼時候打開暖氣的？

▷ Why did you turn on the water?
　你為什麼打開水？

相關用法

turn off

關閉(電燈、瓦斯、音響等)的開關

▷ Did you turn it off?
　你有關掉了嗎？

▷ Did you turn off the ON/OFF switch?
　你有關閉開關了嗎？

▷ Did you turn off the TV?
　你有關掉電視了嗎？

fill out
填寫

▷ Fill out this form.
填寫表格。

▷ Fill out the form, please.
請填寫表格。

▷ Fill out the form below.
填寫以下的表格。

▷ Please fill out the following form.
請填寫以下的表格。

▷ Please fill out the fields in red.
請用紅筆填寫欄位。

▷ Please fill out the blank fields correctly.
請正確地填寫空格。

▷ Could you tell me how to fill out this form?
可以告訴我要如何填寫這個表格嗎?

相關用法

fill in
填寫、填滿

▷ Fill in the blanks with your name.
在空格處填寫你的名字。

▷ Just fill in the application form.
只要填寫申請表格。

▷ Please fill in this claim form.
請填寫這張申訴表。

try on
試穿

▷ I try on this pair of jeans.
我試穿這條牛仔褲。

▷ I'd like to try on this skirt.
我要試穿這件裙子。

▷ I'd like to try on this black skirt.
我要試穿這件黑色的裙子。

▷ I want to try on this shirt.
我想要試穿這件襯衫。

▷ May I try on this one?
我可以試穿這件嗎？

▷ May I try on this coat?
我可以試穿這件外套嗎？

▷ May I try on this pair of shoes?
我可以試穿這雙鞋子嗎？

▷ May I try on this pair of purple sunglasses?
我可以試戴這付紫色太陽眼鏡嗎？

▷ Would you like to try it on?
你要試穿嗎？

▷ Why don't you try on this shirt?
你為什麼不試穿這件襯衫？

▷ You may try on this dress.
你可以試穿這件衣服。

▷ Try on this sweater to see how it looks.
試穿這件毛衣看看效果如何。

▷ Try this jacket on and see if it fits.
試穿這件外套看看合不合身。

▷ You can try it on in the fitting room.
你可以在試衣間裡試穿。

feel like
想要、感到好似

▷ I feel like crying.
我好想哭。

▷ I feel like taking a walk.
我想要散步。

▷ I feel like changing my mind.
我想要改變我的想法。

▷ I feel like having a rest.
我想要休息一下。

▷ I feel like having eggs this morning.
我今天早上想要吃蛋。

▷ I feel like having bacon for dinner tonight.
我今晚的晚餐想要吃培根。

▷ I feel like making something stupid.
我好像做了件蠢事。

▷ I don't feel like studying tonight.
我今晚不想念書。

▷ How do you feel like?
你覺得如何？

▷ I feel like a cup of tea.
我想要喝一杯茶。

▷ Do you feel like a cup of coffee?
你想喝一杯咖啡嗎？

▷ She felt like a fool.
她覺得自己好像是個大笨蛋。

▷ I feel like an idiot.
我覺得自己好像是個傻瓜。

fall for

迷戀、上…的當

▷ I can see why you fell for him.
我能理解你為什麼會迷戀他。

▷ I can't believe you fell for him again.
我不敢相信你又愛上他了。

▷ I wonder why she fell for him.
我懷疑為什麼她會迷戀上他。

▷ She fell for David.
她迷戀上大衛了。

▷ She fell for him at first sight.
她對他一見鍾情。

▷ She fell for that guy because he is cute.
因為那傢伙很帥，她迷戀上他了。

▷ He really fell for the new girl in school.
他深深地被學校新來的女生吸引住了。

▷ Did you fall for her?
你迷戀上她了嗎？

▷ It is the first time you fell for someone?
這是你第一次迷戀上某人嗎？

▷ I fell for her tricks.
我上她的當了。

▷ Don't fall for his tricks.
不要被他的詭計欺騙。

▷ Many people fell for his tricks.
許多人上了他的當。

▷ I set a trap and he fell for it.
我設計了一個陷阱，然後他就上當了。

insist on

堅持、強烈地要求

▷ I insist on having a holiday abroad every year.
我堅持每年出國度假一次。

▷ I insist on taking David to school.
我堅持送大衛去學校。

▷ I insist on going to the doctor right away.
我堅持馬上就去看醫生。

▷ I insist on going to the zoo tomorrow.
我堅持明天去動物園。

▷ I insist on going bicycling.
我堅持要去騎車。

▷ Should I insist on going on vacation?
我應該要堅持去度假嗎？

▷ He insists on going to the beach.
他堅持去海邊。

▷ She insists on taking a risk to save people.
她堅持就算冒險也要去救人。

▷ Why do you insist on having your own business?
為什麼你要堅持擁有自己的事業？

▷ He insisted on his innocence.
他堅持他是無辜的。

▷ We insist on the highest standards of cleanliness in the hotel.
我們堅持飯店有高標準的清潔。

work out
解決、確定、成功、健身

▷ Did you work out the answer yet?
你算出答案了嗎？

▷ Did you work out the sum yet?
你算出總額了嗎？

▷ Try and work out how much it will all cost.
試著算出來會需要多少費用。

▷ I had worked out that it would cost over $100.
我算出來它可能要價超過100元。

▷ I hope the new job works out for you.
希望這個工作對你來說順利。

▷ The sum doesn't work out.
我算不出總額。

▷ I can't work out how to do it.
我實在不知道要如何解決。

▷ I have to work it out.
我必須要解決這件事。

▷ She really wants to work it out with him.
她真的想要和他一起解決它。

▷ We can work it out together.
我們可以一起解決這件事。

▷ She is working out in the gem.
她在健身房健身。

▷ Did you work out?
你有健身嗎？

make sure
確認、確定

▷ I'll just go back and make sure.
我會回去確認。

▷ I want to make sure that you trust me.
我想要確認你是信任我的。

▷ Do you want me to make sure?
你要我去做確認嗎？

▷ Did you make sure?
你有確認了嗎？

▷ Did you make sure for David?
你有幫大衛確認了嗎？

▷ Could you make sure for me?
你能幫我做確認嗎？

▷ Make sure you get there before midnight.
要確認午夜前你抵達那裡。

▷ Make sure that you have enough money with you.
要確認你有帶足夠的錢。

▷ Make sure that she was OK.
要確認她沒問題了。

▷ Make sure that they know how to do it.
要確認他們知道要如何做。

▷ Please make sure you can do it.
請確認你可以辦得到。

▷ Make sure who they are.
要確認他們的身份。

die of
死於(疾病、饑餓、悲傷等的)原因

▷ He died of age.
他壽終正寢。

▷ He died of cancer.
他因為癌症過世。

▷ He died of hunger.
他因為飢餓過世。

▷ He died of heart failure.
他因為心臟衰竭過世。

▷ He died of AIDS in 2004.
他在2004年因為愛滋病過世。

▷ He died of disease in Detroit.
他因病在底特律過世。

▷ He died of lung cancer when I was 12 years old.
當我12歲時，他因為肺癌過世。

相關用法

die from
死於(負傷、衰弱)

▷ He died from an infected wound.
他因為傷口感染過世。

▷ Maria died from a bullet injury.
瑪莉亞因為槍傷過世。

▷ Mr. Smith died from something else.
史密斯先生因為某種其他原因而過世。

look out

小心、注意

▷ Look out!
小心點！

▷ Look out, OK?
小心點，好嗎？

▷ Look out, kids!
小朋友們，小心點！

▷ Look out, boys!
年輕人，小心點！

▷ Look out, you guys!
各位，小心點！

▷ Look out, there is danger ahead.
小心！前面危險。

▷ Look out! There is a car coming.
小心！有一輛車過來了。

▷ Look out! There is a red light up ahead.
小心！前面是紅燈。

相關用法

be careful

小心、注意

▷ Be careful.
小心。

▷ Be careful what you write online.
要小心你在網路的言論。

▷ Be careful not to touch anything.
小心不要碰觸任何東西。

get along with
與...和睦相處、合得來、在...方面進展

▷ He gets along well with his boss.
他和他的老闆相處得很好。

▷ Maria doesn't get along with them.
瑪莉亞和他們處得不好。

▷ He doesn't get along with David.
他和大衛處得不好。

▷ She sometimes doesn't get along with her mom.
有的時候她和她的母親處得不好。

▷ She really doesn't get along with anyone.
她和任何人都處不來。

▷ My dog doesn't get along with my cat.
我的狗和我的貓處得不好。

▷ It's good to get along with your teacher.
能和你的老師處得來是好事。

▷ It's easy to get along well with others.
和其他人處得好是簡單的事。

▷ How to get along with my supervisor?
要如何和我的主管相處？

▷ Do you and your sister get along?
你和你姊妹處得來嗎？

search for
尋找、搜尋(某物)

▷ What are you searching for?
你在找什麼?

▷ We searched for food.
我們有找尋食物。

▷ They searched for him everywhere.
他們到處搜尋他。

▷ I searched for her all over the camp.
我在校園到處找她。

▷ They searched for that young girl.
他們在搜尋那位年輕女孩。

▷ We searched for appropriate buyers.
我們在找尋適合的買方。

▷ He searched his pocket for a cigarette.
他在口袋裏找煙。

相關用法

look for
尋覓

▷ David is looking for his dog.
大衛正在找他的狗。

▷ I'm looking for a job.
我正在找工作。

▷ We looked for a house last year.
我們去年有在找房子。

hand in
交上、上交、交出

▷ Hand in your report.
交出你們的報告。

▷ Remember hand in your homework on time.
記得要準時繳交你們的作業。

▷ Please hand in your essay right away.
請立刻繳交你們的論文。

▷ Hand in your homework by 5 P.M.
在下午五點前繳交你們的作業。

▷ Please hand in your homework no later than 5 P.M.
不要晚於下午五點前繳交你們的作業。

▷ Please hand in your homework on Friday.
請在週五繳交你們的作業。

▷ Listen, boys, hand in your design on Monday.
男孩子們，聽好，請在星期一繳交你們的設計。

▷ Just hand in your essay now, if you did not hand it in last week.
如果你上週沒有交，請現在繳交你們的論文。

▷ Each student has to hand in a term paper at the end of the semester.
學期結束時，每位同學必須交一篇學期論文。

▷ The first thing you should do today is hand in your homework.
你今天要做的第一件事是繳交你的作業。

tell...from
區別、辨別

▷ I can't tell her from the students.
我無法從學生中分辨出她。

▷ I can't tell her from any other child.
我無法從其他孩子中分辨出她。

▷ I can't tell her from her sister.
我分辨不出她和她的姊妹。

▷ I can't tell her from her twin sister.
我分辨不出她和她的孿生姊妹。

▷ I can't tell the difference from them.
我分辨不出他們的不同。

▷ I can't tell the truth from a lie anymore.
我再也無法從謊言中分辨出事實。

▷ I can't tell it from looking at them now.
我現在無法光從目視就分辨出他們。

相關用法

distinguish from
區別、辨別

▷ I can't distinguish A from B.
我無法辨別出 A 與 B。

▷ We should try to distinguish facts from rumors.
我們應該分清事實和傳聞。

carry on
繼續進行…、經營

▷ We carry on our conversations.
我們繼續我們的對話。

▷ I tried to carry on my experiments.
我嘗試過繼續我的研究。

▷ We'll carry on our discussion tomorrow.
我們明天將繼續我們的討論。

▷ We carry on our discussion after lunch.
午餐後我們繼續我們的討論。

▷ We must carry on our work in spite of difficulties.
我們必須不顧困難繼續工作。

▷ Why do we carry on screening?
為什麼我們要繼續掃瞄？

▷ We carry on doing it.
我們繼續做這件事。

▷ We carry on being disappointed.
我們持續失望。

▷ I carry on taking my pills as usual.
我像往常一樣服用我的藥。

▷ The two cities have been carrying on trade for years.
這兩個城市進行貿易已經多年了。

▷ I wish you'd stop carrying on about it.
我希望你停止抱怨。

run into
偶遇、撞到、遭遇

▷ I ran into them in public.
我在公開場中遇到了他們。

▷ I ran into my elder sister yesterday.
我昨天遇到了我的姊姊。

▷ I ran into an old friend of mine in a pub.
我在酒吧遇到了一位老朋友。

▷ I ran into my ex-girlfriend yesterday.
我昨天遇到了我的前女友。

▷ I ran into my ex-husband today.
我今天遇到了我的前夫。

▷ I ran into David at the mall today.
我今天在賣場遇到了大衛。

▷ I ran into the telephone pole.
我撞到了電線桿。

▷ The bus ran into a wall.
公車撞上了牆。

▷ I ran into a little problem.
我遭遇到一個小問題。

▷ I ran into a similar problem yesterday.
昨天我遇到了一個類似的問題。

▷ The project ran into numerous financial difficulties.
這個計畫遭遇到了很多的財務困難。

grow up
成長、逐漸形成

▷ I wish you'd grow up.
希望你成熟點。

▷ I grew up in Taiwan.
我是在台灣長大的。

▷ I grew up in a small town.
我是在一個小城鎮長大的。

▷ I grew up in a Christian family.
我是在一個基督教的家庭長大的。

▷ I was born and grew up in the USA.
我是在美國出生、成長的。

▷ The boys grew up.
孩子們長大了。

▷ My daughter grew up in Seattle.
我的女兒是在西雅圖長大的。

▷ Where did you grow up?
你在哪裡長大的？

▷ I grew up with David.
我是和大衛一起長大的。

▷ What do you want to be when you grow up?
你長大後要做什麼？

▷ A warm friendship grew up between the two men.
兩人之間逐漸產生了友情。

stay up
熬夜

▷ She stayed up reading until midnight.
她熬夜看書看到半夜(才睡)。

▷ We stayed up to watch a film.
我們熬夜看電影。

▷ I stayed up until 2 A.M.
我熬夜到清晨兩點。

▷ We can stay up.
我們可以熬夜。

▷ You should stay up late like me.
你應該像我一樣熬夜。

▷ Why did you stay up?
你為什麼要熬夜？

▷ Don't stay up all night celebrating.
不要徹夜狂歡。

▷ Do you have to stay up so late?
你一定非得熬夜到這麼晚嗎？

▷ If we stay up it will have worked out.
假如我們熬夜，就可以解決事情。

▷ Will you stay up to watch the baseball game?
你會熬夜看棒球賽嗎？

▷ Try not to stay up, will you?
試著不要熬夜，可以嗎？

Part

4

常用生活用語

碰到熟人

▷ Hello.
哈囉！

▷ Hello, guys.
哈囉，各位！

▷ Hello, my friends.
哈囉，我的朋友們。

▷ Hey.
嘿！

▷ Hi, David.
嗨，大衛。

▷ Hi, there.
嗨，你好。

▷ Hi, long time no see.
嗨，好久不見了。

▷ I haven't seen you for ages.
好久不見了！

▷ I haven't seen you for a long time.
好久不見了！

▷ It's been a long time.
好久不見。

▷ It's been so long.
好久不見。

▷ Where have you been?
你都去哪啦？

▷ You haven't changed at all.
你一點都沒變。

問候

▷ Good morning.
早安！

▷ Good afternoon.
午安！

▷ Good evening.
晚安！

▷ Good morning, David.
大衛，早安！

▷ How do you do?
你好嗎？

▷ How are you?
你好嗎？

▷ How are you doing?
你好嗎？

▷ How are you going today?
今天過得如何？

▷ IIow have you been?
你最近怎樣？

▷ How is everything?
你好嗎？

▷ How is it going?
事情都還好吧？

▷ How is your wife?
嫂夫人好嗎？

▷ How is your family?
你的家人好嗎？

▷ How was your day?
今天過得好嗎？

簡單寒暄

▷ You look great.
你看起來氣色不錯！

▷ Are you OK?
你還好吧？

▷ Something wrong?
有事嗎？

▷ Is everything OK?
凡事還好吧？

▷ What's up?
發生什麼事了？

▷ What happened?
發生什麼事了？

▷ What happened to you?
你發生什麼事了？

▷ What have you been doing?
你都在做些什麼？

▷ What's the matter with you?
你發生什麼事了？

▷ What's wrong?
怎麼啦？

▷ What's happening?
發生什麼事？

▷ Where are you off to?
你趕著要去哪裡？

▷ How did it go today?
今天過得如何？

隨口答腔

▷ Great.
很好！

▷ Pretty well.
很好！

▷ I'm doing fine.
我還可以。

▷ I'm doing great.
我過得不錯。

▷ I'm pretty good.
我蠻好的。

▷ I'm fine.
我很好。

▷ I'm OK.
我還過得去。

▷ Nothing special.
沒什麼特別的。

▷ So far so good.
目前為止都還好。

▷ I'm exhausted.
我累壞了！

▷ So-so.
馬馬虎虎！

▷ Not too bad.
不太壞。

▷ Same as usual.
和平常一樣。

認識新朋友

▷ What should I call you?
我要怎麼稱呼你？

▷ What's your name again?
你說你叫什麼名字？

▷ What's your last name?
你貴姓？

▷ And you are?
那你的大名是？

▷ Nice to meet you.
很高興認識你。

▷ Nice to meet you, too.
(我也)很高興認識你。

▷ Nice to see you.
很高興認識你。

▷ Nice to see you, too.
(我也)很高興認識你。

▷ Glad to see you.
很高興認識你。

▷ It's nice to meet you.
很高興認識你。

▷ I'm glad to meet you.
我很高興認識你。

▷ My pleasure to meet you.
能認識你是我的榮幸。

▷ I do know you. David, right?
我認識你。(你是)大衛，對吧？

▷ We have never met before.
我們以前不曾見過面。

介紹自己

▷ I'm David.
我是大衛。

▷ I'm David White.
我是大衛‧懷特。

▷ My name is David.
我的名字是大衛。

▷ Please call me David.
請叫我大衛。

▷ Just call me David.
叫我大衛就好。

▷ David White.
(我是)大衛‧懷特。

▷ David. David White.
(我是)大衛。大衛‧懷特。

▷ David White, by the way.
順帶一提,(我是)大衛‧懷特。

▷ This is my wife Maria.
這是我的太太瑪莉亞。

▷ John, this is my wife Maria.
約翰,這是我太太瑪莉亞。

▷ Come to see my wife Maria.
來見見我的太太瑪莉亞。

▷ My daughter, Jenny. The other is James.
(這是)我的女兒珍妮。另外一個是詹姆士。

▷ I'm David, Maria's husband.
我是大衛,瑪莉亞的先生。

邀請

▷ How about seeing a movie?
要不要去看電影？

▷ How about having dinner with me?
要和我一起吃晚餐嗎？

▷ What are you going to do tonight?
你(們)今晚有要做什麼嗎？

▷ What do you want to do tonight?
你(們)今晚想要做什麼？

▷ Are you doing anything tonight?
你(們)今晚有要做什麼事嗎？

▷ Are you busy tonight?
你(們)今晚忙嗎？

▷ Do you have any plans for tonight?
你(們)今晚有事嗎？

▷ Do you want to come over?
你(們)要來嗎？

▷ Do you want to go out for dinner tonight?
今晚要一起出去吃晚餐嗎？

▷ Would you like to join us?
你(們)要加入我們嗎？

▷ Would you like to hang out with us?
你(們)要和我們出去嗎？

▷ Would you like to see a movie?
你(們)要看電影嗎？

▷ Would you like to come to my party?
你(們)要不要來參加我的派對？

答應

▷ Sounds great.
聽起來不錯。

▷ That's terrific.
不錯啊！

▷ That would be fine.
好啊！

▷ No problem.
沒問題！

▷ Yes.
是的！

▷ OK.
好！

▷ Sure.
可以啊！

▷ Sure. Why not.
好啊！為什麼不要！

▷ Of course.
當然！

▷ No sweat.
沒問題！

▷ I'd love to.
我願意！

▷ Keep going.
繼續(說或做)。

▷ Go ahead.
去做吧！

▷ I'll be there.
我一定會出席。

拒絕

▷ No, thanks.
不用，謝謝！

▷ No, I don't want to.
不，我不想要。

▷ No, I don't think so.
不，我不這麼認為。

▷ No, I won't.
不，我不要。

▷ I'm afraid not.
恐怕不行。

▷ I don't think so.
我不這麼認為。

▷ I don't think this is a good idea.
我覺得這個主意不好！

▷ That's impossible.
不可能！

▷ No way.
想都別想！

▷ Of course not.
當然不好！

▷ Don't think about it.
別想了！

▷ Don't even think about it.
想都別想。

▷ I'd love to but I have other plans.
我很願意，可是我有其他計畫了！

▷ I'll let you know.
我會再告訴你。

感謝

▷ Thanks.
　謝啦！

▷ Thanks a lot.
　多謝啦！

▷ Thanks again.
　再次謝謝！

▷ Thank you.
　謝謝你。

▷ Thank you so much.
　非常謝謝你。

▷ Thank you very much.
　非常謝謝你。

▷ Thank you anyway.
　總之，還是要謝謝你！

▷ Thank you for everything.
　謝謝你為我所做的一切。

▷ It's very nice of you.
　你真好！

▷ I don't know how to thank you.
　我不知道要如何感謝你。

▷ I don't know what to say.
　我真不知道要怎麼說！

▷ I really appreciate it!
　我真的很感激！

▷ I just want to say thank you.
　我只想說謝謝你！

▷ Thank you is not enough.
　太感謝了！

道歉

▷ Sorry.
抱歉。

▷ I'm sorry.
抱歉。

▷ I'm really sorry.
我非常抱歉。

▷ I'm terribly sorry.
我真的非常抱歉。

▷ My mistake.
(這是)我的錯。

▷ My fault.
(這是)我的錯。

▷ It's my fault.
是我的過失。

▷ Will you forgive me?
你願意原諒我嗎？

▷ Please forgive me.
請原諒我。

▷ Please accept my apology.
請接受我的道歉。

▷ I apologize.
我道歉。

▷ You should apologize to Maria.
你應該要向瑪莉亞道歉。

▷ I accept your apology.
我接受你的道歉。

▷ Your apology is not accepted.
我不接受你的道歉。

協助

▷ Help me.
幫幫我。

▷ Please help me.
請幫助我。

▷ Please help me with it.
請幫我一下。

▷ Give me a hand, please.
請幫助我。

▷ I need your help.
我需要你的幫助。

▷ I need some help.
我需要一些幫助。

▷ Please do me a favor.
請幫我一個忙。

▷ Can you help me?
你能幫我嗎？

▷ Would you do me a favor?
你能幫我一個忙嗎？

▷ Are you busy now?
你現在忙嗎？

▷ I don't need your help.
我不需要你的幫助！

▷ Do you need help?
你需要幫忙嗎？

▷ I can help you.
我可以幫你。

祝福

▷ Congratulations.
恭喜！

▷ Good for you.
對你是好的！

▷ Good luck.
祝你好運！

▷ I'm happy for you.
我真為你感到高興！

▷ Cheers.
乾杯！

▷ Have a nice weekend.
週末愉快。

▷ Have a nice time.
祝你快樂。

▷ Take care.
保重。

▷ Take care of yourself.
你自己要保重。

▷ Say hi to David for me.
幫我向大衛問好。

▷ Say hi to him for me.
幫我向他問好。

▷ Tell him I miss him.
告訴他我想念他。

▷ Give my love to David.
幫我向大衛問好。

▷ Give my best to David.
幫我向大衛問好。

道別

▷ Bye.
再見！

▷ Bye for now.
先再見囉！

▷ Goodbye.
再見！

▷ See you.
再見！

▷ See you soon.
再見！

▷ See you around.
再見！

▷ I'll see you later.
再見！

▷ So long.
再見！

▷ Farewell.
再會！

▷ Take care.
保重！

▷ Catch you later.
再見！

▷ Have a nice day.
祝你有美好的一天！

▷ I have to go.
我要走了！

▷ Good night.
晚安！(就寢前使用)

身體不舒服

▷ I'm not feeling well.
我覺得不舒服。

▷ I'm feeling weak.
我覺得很虛弱。

▷ I feel sick.
我覺得生病了！

▷ I feel terrible.
我感覺糟透了！

▷ I feel awful.
我覺得糟透了！

▷ I don't feel well.
我不舒服！

▷ I feel like I'm dying.
我覺得我好像要死了一樣。

▷ I feel sore and ache all over.
我覺得全身痠痛。

▷ I have got a headache.
我頭痛。

▷ I have got a stomachache.
我肚子痛。

▷ I have a fever.
我在發燒。

▷ I sprained my ankle yesterday.
我昨天扭傷我的腳踝。

▷ My shoulder hurts.
我的肩膀痛。

▷ My leg hurts.
我的腳好痛。

感冒

▷ I have the flu.
我感冒了。

▷ I've got a temperature.
我發燒了。

▷ I'm running a high fever.
我發高燒。

▷ I've got a cold.
我感冒了。

▷ I've got a bad cold.
我感冒很嚴重。

▷ I've got a runny nose.
我已經流鼻水了。

▷ My nose is running.
我鼻水流個不停。

▷ I've got a sore throat.
我喉嚨痛。

▷ My throat hurts.
我的喉嚨痛。

▷ I've been coughing day and night.
我早晚都在咳嗽。

▷ I can't stop sneezing.
我噴嚏打個不停。

▷ This headache is killing me.
我頭快痛死了。

▷ I feel dizzy.
我頭暈。

▷ My head is swimming.
我頭昏腦脹的。

關心病患

▷ How do you feel now?
你現在覺得如何？

▷ You look pale.
你(臉色)看起來蒼白！

▷ You really sound sick.
聽起來你真的生病了！

▷ You'd better go home.
你最好回家。

▷ You'd better get some rest.
你最好要多休息。

▷ Did you see a doctor?
你有去看醫生了嗎？

▷ Are you OK?
你還好吧？

▷ You need to lie down.
你最好躺下來(休息)。

▷ Try to get some sleep.
試著睡覺吧！

▷ Stay in bed for a few days.
在床上多躺躺休息幾天。

▷ You should see a doctor.
你應該要去看醫生。

▷ Why don't you see a doctor?
你為什麼不去看醫生？

▷ Did you take medicine?
你有吃藥了嗎？

▷ Let me call an ambulance for you.
讓我幫你叫救護車。

安撫情緒

▷ Come on.
不要這樣！

▷ Give me a hug.
給我一個擁抱。

▷ Take it easy.
放輕鬆。

▷ You need a break.
你需要休息！

▷ Oh, poor David.
喔！可憐的大衛！

▷ God bless you.
上帝(會)保佑你。

▷ Don't worry about it.
不要擔心。

▷ Everything will be fine.
凡事都會沒問題的。

▷ I'm sorry to hear that.
我很遺憾聽見這件事。

▷ I'm here with you.
我在這裡陪著你。

▷ I know how you feel.
我知道你的感受！

▷ You'll get through it.
你會度過難關的。

▷ It's not easy for you.
難為你了。

▷ It must be tough for you.
你一定很不好受！

吵架

▷ Shut up!
閉嘴！

▷ Knock it off.
少來這一套！

▷ Get out of my face.
從我面前消失！

▷ Leave me alone.
走開。／別管我。

▷ Get lost.
滾開！

▷ I hate you!
我討厭你！

▷ I don't want to see your face.
我不要再見到你！

▷ Don't bother me.
別煩我。

▷ Don't give me your shit.
別跟我胡扯！

▷ You piss me off.
你氣死我了！

▷ You're out of your mind.
你腦子有毛病！

▷ You make me sick!
你真讓我覺得噁心！

▷ You're a jerk!
你是個混蛋！

▷ Who do you think you are?
你以為你是誰？

抱怨

▷ That's terrible.
真糟糕！

▷ Enough is enough!
夠了！

▷ Don't push me!
別逼我！

▷ I'm telling you for the last time!
我最後一次告訴你！

▷ I can't take you anymore!
我再也受不了你啦！

▷ I wish I had never met you.
我真後悔這輩子遇到你！

▷ I'll never forgive you!
我永遠都不會饒恕你！

▷ Who do you think you're talking to?
你以為你在跟誰説話？

▷ You're nothing to me.
你對我來説無足輕重。

▷ You're so careless.
你真粗心。

▷ You're away too far.
你太過分了。

▷ You have ruined everything.
你搞砸了一切！

▷ Look at the mess you've made!
看你搞得一團糟！

勸人冷靜

▷ Calm down.
  冷靜點！

▷ Relax.
  放輕鬆！

▷ Take your time.
  慢慢來！

▷ Take it easy.
  放輕鬆點！

▷ Forget it.
  算了！

▷ Just let it be.
  算了吧！

▷ Don't be so mad.
  不要這麼生氣！

▷ Come on, don't be so mad.
  好了啦，不要這麼生氣！

▷ Don't be so angry.
  不要這麼生氣！

▷ It doesn't help.
  沒有幫助的。

▷ It's not your fault.
  這不是你的錯。

▷ What a let down!
  真令人失望！

▷ That's going too far!
  這太離譜了！

▷ It's his lost.
  這是他的損失。

遇到困難

▷ It's impossible.
不可能！

▷ Don't lose your mind.
不要失去理智。

▷ Don't worry about it.
不要擔心！

▷ Don't take it so hard.
看開一點。

▷ Don't panic.
不要慌張。

▷ Just tell me what happened.
只要告訴我發生什麼事了。

▷ Do something.
想想辦法！

▷ You shouldn't work so hard.
你不應該工作得這麼辛苦。

▷ You'd better take a vacation.
你最好休假。

▷ You should eat something.
你應該吃點東西。

▷ You'd better report it to the police.
你最好向警察報案。

▷ You'd better call the bank immediately.
你最好立刻通報銀行。

▷ You really ought to move out.
你真的應該搬出去。

▷ What I would do is call the police.
我會做的是打電話報警。

想辦法解決

▷ Try again.
再試一次！

▷ Do your best.
你要盡力！

▷ Use your head.
動動腦想一想！

▷ Find your own way.
用你自己的方法。

▷ See? It's easy.
看吧！很簡單！

▷ It's not hard.
這不難！

▷ It's your decision.
這是你的決定。

▷ It's your responsibility.
這是你的責任。

▷ You should try to figure it out.
你應該試著想辦法解決。

▷ Do you want my advice?
需要我的建議嗎？

▷ Aren't you going to do something?
你不想辦法嗎？

▷ Why don't you try to do it?
你為什麼不試著做這件事？

▷ This is how you can do.
你可以這麼做。

▷ I want to offer a suggestion.
我想要提供一個建議！

提議

▷ May I help you?
需要我幫忙嗎？

▷ How about this one?
這個怎麼樣？

▷ Just think about it.
可以考慮看看吧！

▷ I have an idea.
我有一個主意。

▷ You should go out and do something.
你應該要出去找點事做。

▷ Why don't we go out for dinner?
我們何不出去吃晚餐？

▷ Why don't we go for a walk?
我們何不出去走走？

▷ Why don't we go for a drive?
我們何不開車出去兜兜風？

▷ How about hanging out with me?
要不要和我出去逛逛？

▷ How do you like going to a concert?
你要不要去聽演唱會？

▷ Maybe we can go to a movie.
也許我們可以去看電影。

▷ Do you want to go to a movie?
你想去看電影嗎？

▷ Would you like to join me?
要不要一起去？

▷ Come on. That would be fun.
來嘛！會很好玩的！

讚美

▷ Good job.
幹得好！

▷ Well done.
幹得好！

▷ Cool.
酷喔！

▷ Excellent.
真是不錯！

▷ Fantastic.
太好了！

▷ Terrific.
太好了！

▷ Brilliant.
很讚喔！

▷ Nice dress.
不錯的衣服喔！

▷ Nice tie.
不錯的領帶喔！

▷ Good for you.
(這)對你來說很好。

▷ That was very smart.
很聰明！

▷ Smart girl.
聰明的女孩！

▷ You are doing well.
你表現得很好！

▷ You are so great.
你很棒！

失望

▷ I'm so disappointed.
我好失望！

▷ I'm not myself.
我感覺不好！

▷ I feel frustrated.
我覺得很沮喪。

▷ I feel terrible.
我覺得糟透了！

▷ I feel sad.
我很難過！

▷ I screwed up.
我搞砸了！

▷ I don't think it's a good idea.
我不覺得是個好主意。

▷ You make me down.
你讓我很失望！

▷ You hurt me so hard.
你傷我好深！

▷ You are wasting my time.
你在浪費我的時間！

▷ How could you do that?
你怎麼能這麼做？

▷ Too bad.
太糟了！

▷ My God.
我的天啊！

詢問意見

▷ What do you think?
你認為呢？

▷ What's your advice?
你的建議呢？

▷ What's your opinion?
你的意見呢？

▷ How about this one?
這一個如何？

▷ Don't you think so?
你不這麼認為嗎？

▷ Why not?
為什麼不行？

▷ How come?
為什麼？

▷ Just tell me why?
只要告訴我為什麼？

▷ What's your reason?
你的理由是什麼？

▷ Why did you do that?
你為什麼這麼做？

▷ Why did you say that?
你為什麼這麼說？

▷ What makes you think so?
你為什麼會這麼認為？

▷ Is there a reason?
有理由嗎？

▷ What for?
為了什麼？

同情

▷ It's not your fault.
不是你的錯！

▷ It's no problem.
這不是問題。

▷ It happens.
難免會發生。

▷ It will work out.
事情會解決的！

▷ That's all right.
沒關係的！

▷ I'm sorry to hear that.
我很遺憾知道這件事。

▷ I hope it's nothing serious.
希望情況不會太嚴重。

▷ How awful!
真是不幸啊！

▷ How terrible!
真是悲慘啊！

▷ What a pity!
真是可惜啊！

▷ Gee, that's too bad!
真是太糟了啊！

▷ Poor baby.
可憐的孩子！

▷ Poor guy.
可憐的傢伙！

▷ Don't blame yourself.
不要自責！

鼓勵

▷ Go for it.
加油！

▷ Cheer up.
高興點！

▷ Oh, come on.
喔，不要這樣。

▷ Keep going.
繼續努力！

▷ Make me proud of you.
要讓我以你為榮。

▷ Use your gift.
善用你的天賦！

▷ Prove it.
拿出證明！

▷ Prove yourself to me.
向我證明你自己(的能力)！

▷ You can do it.
你可以做得到的！

▷ It's no problem to you, right?
對你而言是沒問題的，對吧？

▷ Don't give up.
不要放棄！

▷ Don't underestimate yourself.
不要低估自己的能力！

▷ Don't put yourself down.
不要瞧不起自己！

▷ Where is your ambition?
你的雄心壯志在哪裡？

認同

▷I agree with you.
我同意你。

▷I agree.
我同意。

▷Bingo.
答對了！

▷That's it.
沒錯。

▷You got it.
就是如此。

▷Correct.
正確的。／沒錯！

▷Count me in.
把我算進去。

▷I'm on your side.
我是站在你這邊的。

▷Never mind.
不用在意。

▷It's OK.
沒關係。

▷It's no big deal.
沒什麼大不了。

▷I see.
我瞭解！

▷I understand.
我瞭解！

▷I think so, too.
我也是這麼認為！

去電找人

▷Is David there?
大衛在嗎？

▷Is David around?
大衛在嗎？

▷Is David in today?
大衛今天在嗎？

▷Is David there, please?
請問大衛在嗎？

▷Is David in the office now?
大衛現在在辦公室裡嗎？

▷I need to talk to David.
我要和大衛講電話。

▷I'd like to talk to David.
我要和大衛講電話。

▷This is James calling for David.
我是詹姆士打電話來要找大衛。

▷Hello, may I speak to David?
哈囉，我能和大衛講電話嗎？

▷May I speak to David, please?
我能和大衛講電話嗎？

▷Could I talk to David or Sunny?
我能和大衛或桑尼講電話嗎？

▷Hi, David?
嗨，大衛嗎？

▷Hi, David? This is John.
嗨，大衛？我是約翰。

▷This is David calling. Is Jenny around?
我是大衛。珍妮在嗎？

回電

▷ I'm returning your call.
我現在回你電話。

▷ You called me last night, didn't you?
你昨晚有打電話給我，不是嗎？

▷ Thank you for returning my call.
謝謝你回我電話。

▷ That's all right. I'll try to call him later.
沒關係。我晚一點再打電話給他。

▷ I'll try again later.
我晚一點再試一次(打電話)。

▷ I'll return his call.
我會回他的電話。

▷ I'll call back again.
我會再打電話來。

▷ I'll call you back later.
我待會會回電話給你。

▷ When should I call back then?
那我應該什麼時候回電？

▷ Can I call again in 10 minutes?
我可以十分鐘後再打電話過來嗎？

▷ Call me back, OK?
回電給我好嗎？

▷ Would you tell him I called?
可以告訴他我來電過嗎？

▷ Tell him to call me back.
告訴他回我電話。

▷ I'll have him call you back.
我會請他回你電話。

接電話

▷ Speaking.
請說。

▷ This is David Smith.
我是大衛・史密斯。

▷ This is she.
我就是你要找的人。(適用女性)

▷ This is he.
我就是你要找的人。(適用男性)

▷ It's me.
我就是。

▷ I can't talk to you now.
我現在不能講電話。

▷ I'm really busy now.
我現在真的很忙。

▷ I'm sorry, but he is busy with another line.
很抱歉,他正在忙線中。

▷ Would you mind calling back later?
你介意稍後再打電話過來嗎?

▷ Wait a moment, please. I'll get him.
請稍等。我去叫他。

▷ Who is calling, please?
你是哪一位?

▷ May I ask who is calling, please?
請問你是哪一位?

▷ I'll connect you.
我幫你轉接電話。

▷ You can try again in a few minutes.
你可以過幾分鐘後再打電話過來。

請來電者稍候

▷ Hold on, please.
請稍等。

▷ Hold the line, please.
請稍等不要掛斷電話。

▷ Hang on a second.
稍等。

▷ Wait a moment.
等一下。

▷ Just a minute, please.
請等一下。

▷ Can you hold?
你能等嗎？

▷ Could you wait a moment, please?
能請你稍候片刻嗎？

▷ Would you mind holding for one minute?
你介意稍候片刻嗎？

▷ Could you hold the line, please?
能請你稍等不要掛斷電話嗎？

▷ Would you like to hold?
你要等一下嗎？

▷ Would you like to hang on?
請別掛斷好嗎？

▷ Could you hold for another minute?
你能再等一下嗎？

▷ The line is busy, would you like to hang on?
電話佔線中，請別掛斷好嗎？

詢問來電者身份

▷ Who is this?
你是哪位？

▷ Who is this, please?
請問你的大名？

▷ May I ask who is calling?
請問你的大名？

▷ May I know who is calling?
請教你的大名？

▷ May I have your name, please?
請問你的大名？

▷ Who is calling, please?
請問你的大名？

▷ Who is speaking, please?
請問你的大名？

▷ Whom I'm speaking with?
我正在跟誰講話呢？

▷ Who should I say is calling?
我應該要說是誰來電？

▷ Your name, please?
請問你的大名？

▷ Mr. Smith?
(是)史密斯先生嗎？

▷ And you are?
你是？

▷ Are you Mr. Smith?
你是史密斯先生嗎？

▷ You are...?
你是…？

轉接電話

▷ Extension 701, please.
請接分機701。

▷ May I have extension 701, please?
可以幫我接分機701嗎？

▷ I'll connect you.
我會幫你轉接電話。

▷ I'm transferring your call.
我幫你轉接電話。

▷ I'm redirecting your call.
我幫你轉接電話。

▷ I'm connecting you now.
我現在就幫你轉接電話過去。

▷ I'll put you through.
我會幫你轉接過去。

▷ I'll transfer your call.
我會幫你轉接電話。

▷ I'll put him on.
我會把電話轉接給他。

▷ I'll put her on.
我會把電話轉接給她。

▷ I'll put David on.
我會把電話轉接給大衛。

▷ I'll transfer your call to Mr. Smith.
我會轉接你的電話給史密斯先生。

▷ I'll connect you to extension 701.
我會幫你轉接到分機701。

▷ I'll connect your call to extension 701.
我會幫你轉接到分機701。

留言

▷ Let me take a message.
我來(幫你)記下留言。

▷ What do you want me to tell him?
要我轉達什麼給他嗎？

▷ Would you like to leave a message?
你要留言嗎？

▷ Could I leave him a message?
我能留言給他嗎？

▷ Is there any message?
有沒有要留言？

▷ Let me write down your message.
我來寫下你的留言。

▷ Do you want him to return your call?
你要他回你電話嗎？

▷ Does he have your number?
他知道你的號碼嗎？

▷ How can he get a hold of you?
他要怎麼和你聯絡？

▷ My number is 86473663.
我的號碼是 86473663。

▷ Would you ask him to call David at 86473663?
你能請他打電話到 86473663 給大衛嗎？

▷ Tell him to give me a call as soon as possible.
告訴他盡快回我電話。

逛街

▷ I'm just looking.
我只是隨便看看。

▷ I'm just browsing.
我只是參觀看看。

▷ I'm interested in those gloves.
我對那一些手套有興趣。

▷ I want to buy the earrings.
我想要買耳環。

▷ I need a pair of red gloves.
我需要一雙紅色的手套。

▷ I need to buy birthday presents for my wife.
我需要買生日禮物給我太太。

▷ I'm looking for some skirts.
我正在找一些裙子。

▷ Do you have any purple hats?
你們有紫色的帽子嗎？

▷ Do you have any red ones?
你們有紅色的嗎？

▷ It's a present for my daughter.
是給我女兒的禮物。

▷ They are suitable for my daughters.
他們是很適合我的女兒們。

▷ They look nice.
他們看起來都不錯。

選購商品

▷Do you have any red shirts?
你們有賣紅色的襯衫嗎?

▷I'm interested in this computer.
我對這台電腦有興趣。

▷I need some apples.
我需要一些蘋果。

▷I'd like some pears, too.
我也要買一些梨子。

▷I'd like to see some ties.
我想看一些領帶。

▷May I see those MP3 players?
我能看那些 MP3 播放器嗎?

▷May I have a look at them?
我能看一看它們嗎?

▷Can you show me something different?
你能給我看一些不一樣的嗎?

▷Do you have anything better?
你們有沒有好一點的?

▷Is that all?
全部就這些嗎?

▷Anything else?
還有其他的嗎?

▷This is what I need.
這就是我需要的。

▷It's not what I need.
這不是我需要的(商品)。

▷It's not what I'm looking for.
我不是要找這一種。

選購特定商品

▷ Show me that pen.
給我看那支筆。

▷ Show me that black sweater.
給我看看那件黑色毛衣。

▷ This one is great.
這一個不錯。

▷ They look great.
他們看起來不錯。

▷ Those skirts look great.
那些裙子看起來不錯。

▷ This is what I'm looking for.
我就是在找這一種。

▷ That's what I want.
那就是我要的。

▷ I want this one.
我要這一種。

▷ I think that's what I want.
我想那就是我要的。

▷ I'd like to buy some gloves.
我想要買一些手套。

▷ I don't like this one.
我不喜歡這一件。

▷ Do you have any hats like this one?
你們有沒有像這頂的帽子？

▷ Do you have anything like this one?
有沒有像這個的商品？

▷ Do you have anything like that one?
有沒有像那個的商品？

試穿衣物

▷ Can I try it on?
我可以試穿嗎？

▷ Can I try this on?
我可以試穿這一件嗎？

▷ Can I try this on, too?
我也可以試穿這一件嗎？

▷ May I try on that one, too?
我也可以試穿那一件嗎？

▷ Where is the fitting room?
試衣間在哪裡？

▷ I'd like to try this coat on and see if it fits.
我想試穿這件外套，看看是否合身。

▷ I'll try on a small.
我要試穿小號的。

▷ I'll try on size 8.
我要試穿 8 號。

▷ I need a fourteen.
我需要 14 號。

▷ Do you have this color in size 8?
這個顏色有 8 號的嗎？

▷ Do you have these shoes in size 7?
這些鞋子你有 7 號的嗎？

▷ I should try another bigger one.
我應該要試穿另一件大一點的。

▷ This size is fine.
這個尺寸可以。

▷ This is not my size.
這不是我的尺寸。

試穿結果

▷ Could I try a larger one?
我可以試穿大一點的嗎？

▷ Can I try a smaller one?
我能試穿較小件的嗎？

▷ Don't you think it's too loose?
你不覺得太寬鬆嗎？

▷ The waist was a little tight.
腰部有一點緊。

▷ It feels fine.
感覺不錯。

▷ It feels tight.
有一點緊。

▷ Not bad.
不錯。

▷ It's good, isn't?
不錯，對吧？

▷ It looks perfect to me.
這個我喜歡。

▷ I don't think this is good.
我不覺得這件好。

▷ Do you have this shirt in size 38?
這件襯衫有沒有 38 號的尺寸？

▷ How does this one look on me?
我穿這一件的效果怎麼樣？

▷ It looks great on me.
我穿看起來不錯。

▷ It looks OK on you.
你穿看起來不錯。

售價

▷ How much?
多少錢？

▷ How much is it?
這個多少錢？

▷ How much is this, please?
請問這個要多少錢？

▷ How much is it together?
總共要多少錢？

▷ How much are those apples?
那些蘋果要多少錢？

▷ How much does it cost?
這個要賣多少錢？

▷ How much did you say?
你說要多少錢？

▷ How much shall I pay for it?
這個我應該付多少錢？

▷ How much shall I pay for this one and that one?
這一件和那一件我應該付多少錢？

▷ What is the price for this camera?
這台相機多少錢？

▷ It's too expensive.
它太貴了。

▷ Is it expensive?
會很貴嗎？

▷ Don't you think it's too expensive?
你不覺得太貴了嗎？

議價

▷ Too expensive!
太貴了！

▷ So expensive?
這麼貴？

▷ Can you lower the price?
你可以算便宜一點嗎？

▷ Can you give me a discount?
你可以給我折扣嗎？

▷ Can you give me a 10 percent discount?
你能給我九折嗎？

▷ How about a 10 percent discount?
可以算九折嗎？

▷ Is there a discount for two?
買兩件可以有折扣吧？

▷ Are there any discounts?
有沒有折扣？

▷ No discount?
沒有折扣嗎？

▷ Can you lower the price a bit if I buy them?
如果我買它們，你可以算便宜一點嗎？

▷ Can you make it cheaper?
可以算便宜一點嗎？

▷ Can you lower it four hundred?
可以便宜四百(元)嗎？

▷ How about 2 thousand dollars?
可以算兩千元嗎？

▷ I don't think I can afford it.
我不覺得我付擔得起！

購買

▷ I'll take it.
我要買它。

▷ I'll buy it.
我要買它。

▷ I'll buy these apples.
我要買這些蘋果。

▷ I'll take those apples.
我要買那些蘋果。

▷ I'll get this one.
我要買這一件。

▷ I'll take the small ones.
我要買小的。

▷ I'll take the smaller ones.
我要買較小的。

▷ I'll take the big ones.
我要買大的。

▷ I'll take the bigger ones.
我要買較大的。

▷ I want both of them.
它們兩個我都要。

▷ I want two of these skirts.
我要買這兩件裙子。

▷ No, I'll pass this time.
不要，我這次不買。

▷ Not for this time.
這次先不要(買)。

▷ I don't need any.
我都不需要。

付款

▷ Cash, please.
用現金,麻煩你了。

▷ Credit card, please.
用信用卡(付款),麻煩你了。

▷ I'll pay it by cash.
我要付現金。

▷ With traveler's check.
用旅行支票(付款)。

▷ Do you accept credit cards?
你們接受信用卡付款嗎?

▷ Can I use VISA?
我可以用 VISA 卡嗎?

▷ Do you accept VISA?
你們接受 VISA 卡嗎?

▷ Do you take Master'?
你們接受萬事達卡嗎?

▷ Can I pay in US dollars?
我可以用美金付嗎?

時間

▷ What time?
　幾點？

▷ What time is it now?
　現在幾點了？

▷ Does anyone know what time it is?
　有誰知道幾點了嗎？

▷ Do you have the time?
　你知道(現在)幾點鐘了嗎？

▷ It's ten thirty.
　十點半。

▷ It's twenty after two.
　兩點二十分

▷ It's ten to five.
　四點五十分。

▷ Oh, it's too late.
　喔，太晚了。

▷ Time is running out!
　沒有時間了！

▷ Hurry up. We're late.
　快一點！我們遲到了。

▷ What day is it?
　今天星期幾？

▷ It's Friday.
　是星期五。

▷ What's the date today?
　今天幾月幾日？

▷ It's September second.
　是九月二日。

Part

5

基本句型

Let me try.

讓我試一試！

句型 let + | me, him, her, them, you, us | + 原形動詞

A Let me try.
讓我試一試！

B No, I won't let you do it.
不行。我不會讓你這麼做。

A Let him do it.
讓他去做。

B Why? He's so young.
為什麼？他還這麼年輕。

A What did you say?
你說什麼？

B Let them eat cake.
讓他們吃餅乾。

A I'll let you go.
我會讓你走。

B OK. See you.
好的。再見！

A Let David play the baseball.
讓大衛玩棒球吧！

B OK. Have fun.
好！好好玩吧！

A Put on your socks and shoes.
穿上你的襪子和鞋子。

B OK. Let's go.
好的。我們走吧！

Yes, I do.

是的，我是。/我有。

句型　Yes, +
| I, we, they + do, did |
| she, he, David, it + does, did |

A
Do you read books?
你有唸書嗎？

B
Yes, I do.
是的，我有。

A
Do you listen to the radio?
你有聽收音機嗎？

B
Yes, I do.
是的，我有。

A
Does David make an appointment?
大衛有預約嗎？

B
Yes, he does.
是的，他有。

A
Did you have fun?
你們玩得開心嗎

B
Yes, we did.
是的，我們有。

A
Does he visit you?
他有拜訪你嗎？

B
Yes, he does.
是的，他有。

A
Did the Smiths know about you?
史密斯家人知道你嗎？

B
Yes, they did.
是的，他們知道。

I'd like to see a movie.

我想要去看電影。

句型 I'd like + to + 原形動詞

A I'd like to see a movie.
我想要去看電影。

B Can I join you?
我可以一起去嗎？

A I'd like to have a glass of orange juice.
我要一杯柳橙汁。

B Sure. I'll be right back with you.
好的。我馬上拿給你。

A What would you like your steak?
你要幾分熟的牛排？

B I'd like to have my steak done medium.
我要我的牛排五分熟。

A What would you like?
你想要什麼？

B I'd like to take this one.
我想要這一個。

A I'd like to have a word with you.
我想和你談一談。

B Have a seat.
坐下吧！

A I'd like to have a seat by the window.
我要在窗邊的位置。

B I'll see what I can do.
我來看看有什麼辦法可以做。

You look great.

你看起來氣色很好。

句型 look + (like) + 形容詞

A You look great.
你看起來氣色不錯。

B Thanks. I just got married last month.
謝啦！我上個月才結婚的。

A You look upset.
你看起來很沮喪。

B I didn't pass my exams.
我沒有通過考試。

A You look pale. What's wrong?
你看起來臉色蒼白。怎麼了？

B I am not felling well.
我覺得不舒服。

A You look awful.
你看起來糟透了！

B You are telling me.
還用你說。

A Helen looks like upset. Is she OK?
海倫看起來很沮喪。她還好吧？

B I don't think so.
我不這麼認為。

A They don't look very happy.
他們看起來很不快樂。

B Because they didn't win the game.
因為他們沒有打贏比賽。

Keep going.

繼續(說、做)。

句型 keep + 動名詞
形容詞

A	Can I ask you a question? 我可以問你一個問題嗎？
B	Keep going. 説吧！
A	Shall we slow down? 我們應該要慢一點嗎？
B	No. Keep moving. 不用。繼續前進。
A	You look awful. Are you OK? 你看起來糟透了。你還好吧？
B	No. He kept asking me questions. 不好。他老是問我問題。
A	How did it go? 事情怎麼樣了？
B	It keeps getting worse. 越來越糟了！
A	How is Maria? 瑪莉亞好嗎？
B	She keeps getting better. 她越來越好了！
A	Please keep quiet. 請保持安靜。
B	Yes, madam. 是的，夫人。

I stop drinking.

我戒酒了。

句型 stop + 動名詞

A Is it raining now?
現在有下雨嗎？

B No, it has stopped raining.
沒有，雨已經停了。

A They stop calling me.
他們不再打電話給我。

B What happen to them?
他們怎麼了？

A Why do they stop using it?
他們為什麼不再使用？

B How should I know?
我怎麼會知道？

A Why do you stop reading?
你為什麼不再唸書？

B Because I'm getting sleepy.
因為我有點睏。

A What did the doctor say?
醫生說了什麼？

B He said I should stop drinking.
他說我應該戒酒。

A They stop working in a few hours.
他們幾個小時後就停止工作了。

B How come? What are they trying to do?
為什麼？他們要做什麼？

I don't want any trouble.

我不希望有任何麻煩。

句型 any + 可數名詞複數 / 不可數名詞

A I don't want any trouble.
我不希望有任何麻煩。

B But you are asking for trouble.
但是你是在自找麻煩。

A Could we get any more juice?
我們可以再多要果汁嗎？

B Sure. How about apple juice?
當然可以。蘋果汁可以嗎？

A Can I get any discount?
可以有折扣嗎？

B Yes, you can.
是的，你可以。

A What shall I do?
我該怎麼辦？

B Just send me any data you can find.
只要把你能找到的所有資料送來給我。

A I haven't any money to spare.
我的錢都用光了。

B Where is your money?
你的錢呢？

A If there is any trouble, do let me know.
如果遇到任何麻煩，請務必告訴我。

B Thanks, I will.
謝謝，我會的。

I'm about to find it out!

我會去查出來！

句型 be 動詞 + about + to + 原形動詞

A What's your plan?
你的計畫是什麼？

B I guess I'm about to find it out!
我猜我會去查出來！

A I am about to leave now.
我現在要走了。

B OK. I'll walk you home.
好。我陪你走回家。

A Something terrible is about to happen.
有可怕的事情要發生了。

B What? What terrible thing?
什麼？什麼可怕的事情？

A How is David?
大衛好嗎？

B He is about to quit his job.
他快要辭職。

A He is about to retire.
他就要退休。

B But he is only fifty years old.
但是他才只有五十歲。

A The concert is about to begin.
音樂會快要開始。

B Hurry up. We're getting late.
快一點。我們要遲到了。

I'm going to pick her up.
我會去接她。

句型 be 動詞 + going to + 原形動詞 +(時間狀態)

A I'm going to go to Japan next week!
我下星期要去日本。

B Wow, you are so lucky.
哇，你真幸運。

A How about Maria?
瑪莉亞呢？

B I'm going to pick her up tonight.
我今晚會去接她。

A What are you going to do at the party?
在派對上你們要做什麼？

B We're going to sing at the party.
我們將會在派對上唱歌。

A Look at this car!
看這輛車！

B It's going to crash into the yellow one.
它快要撞上黃色(的車)了。

A What are you going to do?
你要做什麼？

B I'm going to read the book.
我要去念書。

A Are you going to play handball?
你要去玩手球嗎？

B Yes, I am.
是的，我要。

It's right around the corner!

(某個日子)就快到了。

句型

節日
季節　+ be 動詞 + right around the corner
事件

A Summer is right around the corner.
夏天快來了！

B I really don't like the summer time.
我真的不喜歡夏天。

A Spring training is right around the corner.
春訓快要開始了。

B Wow, it won't be an easy job.
哇，不會是簡單的工作。

A Baseball season is right around the corner.
棒球季快要開始了。

B Yeah. I'm getting so nervous.
是啊！我好緊張。

A April is right around the corner.
四月就要到了！

B My birthday is right around the corner too.
我生日也快要到了！

A June 6th is right around the corner.
六月六日就要到了！

B Why? Why do you say so?
為什麼？你為什麼這麼說？

It's getting late.
越來越晚了！

句型 be 動詞 + getting + 形容詞 / 形容詞比較級

A It's getting late.
越來越晚了！

B Yeah, it's about to leave now.
是啊，現在是該走了！

A It's getting worse.
越來越糟！

B Why? What's wrong?
為什麼？怎麼啦？

A How is it going?
事情怎麼樣了？

B It's getting better.
越來越好！

A How is the weather?
天氣怎麼樣？

B It's getting hot out there.
外面越來越熱！

A It's a beautiful day, isn't it?
天氣真好，對嗎？

B Yeap. It's getting windy.
是啊！開始有風了。

A What's the matter with you and Maria?
你和瑪莉亞怎麼啦？

B It's getting complicated.
越來越複雜！

I called you last night.

我昨天晚上有打電話給你。

句型 動詞過去式 + 過去的時間

A When did you call me?
你什麼時候打電話給我的？

B I called you last night.
我昨天晚上有打電話給你。

A What did you eat two days ago?
你二天前吃了什麼？

D I just ate a sandwich two days ago.
我二天前只有吃三明治。

A What did you do last weekend?
你們上個週末做了什麼事？

B We went to see a movie last weekend.
我們上週末去看電影。

A Where do you live now?
你現在住在哪裡？

B Seattle. I just moved back last month.
西雅圖。我上個月剛搬回去。

A Did you make breakfast yesterday?
你昨天有做早餐嗎？

B Yes, I made breakfast yesterday.
沒有，我昨天有做早餐。

I'll see how it goes.

我會看看事情的發展。

句型 see + wh-子句 / how 子句

A What do you say, mom?
媽，妳說呢？

B I'll see how it goes.
我會看看事情的發展。

A Don't you think he is your Mr. Right?
妳不覺得他是你的真命天子嗎？

B I'll see how he does.
我會看看他怎麼做。

A It is your chance, isn't it?
這是你的機會，不是嗎？

B Sure, I'll see what I can do.
當然，我會視情況看我能做什麼。

A Can you help me with it?
你可以幫我嗎？

B No problem. I'll see what I can get you.
沒問題。我看看我能幫你拿什麼來。

A What will they do?
他們會怎麼做？

B They'll see how much you pay.
他們會視你月付多少錢(來決定)。

A What shall I do now?
我現在該怎麼辦？

B You'll see how it works.
你先看看它怎麼運作的。

I saw him on Sunday.
我星期天有看見他。

句型 on + 星期

A On Friday I did an unexpected thing.
星期五我做了一件很不可思議的事。

B What did you do?
你做了什麼事？

A When did you see David?
你什麼時候有看見大衛？

B I saw David on Wednesday.
我星期三有看見大衛。

A I'll pick you up on Friday night.
我會在星期五晚上來接你。

B OK. See you then.
好的。到時候見。

A What did you do on Saturday?
你們星期六做了什麼事？

B We visited my family on Saturday.
我們星期六去拜訪我的家人。

A What do you usually do on Friday?
你通常在星期五做什麼？

B I usually eat dinner with friends.
我通常和朋友吃晚餐。

A What's your plan?
你的計畫是什麼？

B I'll move back to Taipei on Sunday.
我會在星期天搬回台北。

I'll be there on time.
我會準時到達那裡的。

句型 主詞 + 動詞 + on time

A David is always on time for work.
大衛總是準時上班。

B I'm sure he is.
我相信他是的。

A Remember to hand in the report on time.
記得要準時交報告。

B I will.
我會的。

A Will the train arrive on time?
火車會準時到達嗎？

B I don't think so.
我不這麼認為。

A I'll be there on time.
我會準時到達那裡的。

B Good. See you then.
很好。到時候見。

A Will you arrive at school on time?
你會準時到學校嗎？

B I'll do my best.
我會盡量。

A Please attend the meeting on time.
請準時參加會議。

B OK. I'll be there on time.
好的。我會準時到達。

What have I done?

我做了什麼事？

句型 have / has + V p.p.

A Look what you have done?
看看你做了什麼事？

B What have I done?
我做了什麼事？

A Did you do your homework?
你有做你的功課嗎？

B Yes, I have finished it last night.
有的，我昨晚就做完(功課)了。

A Have you called Mr. Smith this morning?
你今天早上有打電話給史密斯先生嗎？

B No, I haven't called him.
沒有，我沒有打電話給他。

A What's David's decision?
大衛的決定是什麼？

B David has decided to study abroad.
大衛已經決定要去國外唸書。

A Do you know about it?
你知道這件事嗎？

B I haven't heard it before.
我以前沒有聽說過。

A Where is David?
大衛在哪裡？

B I haven't seen David for a long time.
我好久沒有見到大衛了。

I was wondering why she called me.

我在想她為什麼打電話給我。

句型 be 動詞過去式 + wondering + wh-子句 / how 子句

A I was wondering why you came back.
我在想你為什麼回來？

B Because I just quit my job.
因為我剛辭掉我的工作。

A I was wondering why she called me.
我在想她為什麼打電話給我。

B You tell me.
你說呢？

A We were wondering what happened to her.
我們在想她發生什麼事了。

B Nothing at all.
沒事啊！

A David was wondering where to go.
大衛在想要去哪裡。

B It's up to him.
由他自己決定。

A He was wondering how to be there on time.
他在想要如何準時到達那裡。

B How about taking a taxi?
要不要搭計程車？

I came from Taiwan.

我來自台灣。

句型　come from + 某地 / 某處

A **Where were you from?**
你來自哪裡？

B **I came from Taiwan.**
我來自台灣。

A **What city did you come from?**
你們來自哪一個城市？

B **We came from Seattle.**
我們來自西雅圖。

A **Where do they come from?**
他們來自哪裡？

B **They come from the USA.**
他們來自美國。

A **Where does Maria come from?**
瑪莉亞來自哪裡？

B **She comes from Virginia.**
她來自維吉尼亞州。

A **Where do you come from?**
你們來自哪裡？

B **David and I came from China.**
大衛和我來自中國。

A **Where does your food come from?**
你(們)的食物從哪裡來的？

B **It's from our school.**
來自於學校。

What is your plan?

你的計畫是什麼？

句型 What + be 動詞 + 所有格 + 名詞

A What is your plan?
你的計畫是什麼？

B I have no idea about it.
我完全沒有概念。

A What is her address?
她的地址是哪裡？

B Sorry, I have no idea.
抱歉，我不知道。

A What is his name?
他的名字是什麼？

B He is David White.
他是大衛・懷特。

A What is your idea?
你的想法是什麼？

B I think we should just let her go.
我覺得我們應該要讓她走。

A What is your problem?
你怎麼了？

B Why? Did I do something wrong?
為什麼(這麼問)？我有做錯事嗎？

A What is your favorite animal?
你最喜歡的動物是什麼？

B My favorite animal is dolphin.
我最喜歡的動物是海豚。

What did you just say?

你剛剛說什麼？

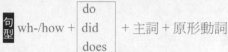

句型 wh-/how + do / did / does + 主詞 + 原形動詞

A You scared the shit out of me.
你嚇得我失禁。

B What did you just say?
你剛剛說什麼？

A What did you just say?
你剛剛說什麼？

B I said you scared me.
你說你嚇壞我了。

A What did they tell you about me?
他們怎麼向你描述我的？

B They said you are the best one.
他們說你是最佳人選。

A How does she look like?
她看起來長什麼樣子？

B She looks so sexy.
她看起來很性感。

A What does he mean by that?
他那是什麼意思？

B How should I know?
我怎麼會知道？

A Where did they find David?
他們在哪裡找到大衛的？

B It's at the library.
在圖書館。

I don't know.

我不知道。

句型 know +
受詞
wh-子句
about +名詞

A **What are they going to do?**
他們要做什麼？

B I don't know anything about it.
我完全不知道。

A **Hey, would you lend me 10 bucks?**
嘿，你可以借我10塊錢嗎？

B No way. I don't even know you.
想都別想了！我又不認識你。

A **I think it's his fault.**
我覺得是他的錯。

B I don't know what you're talking about.
我不知道你在說什麼。

A **Why did they say that?**
他們為什麼要這麼說？

B I don't know why they said so.
我不知道他們為什麼這麼說。

A **What the hell is going on here?**
這裡到底發生什麼事了？

B I don't know about anything.
我完全不知道。

You wanna fight?

你想要吵架嗎？

句型 wanna (= want to) + 原形動詞

A Do you wanna play game?
你想要玩遊戲嗎？

B Sure. Why not.
當然好。為什麼不要。

A Do you wanna go to bed?
你想要上床睡覺嗎？

B Yes, I am so cxhausted.
好啊，我好累喔！

A I wanna play a game.
我想要玩遊戲。

B You should clean up your room first.
你應該要先清理你的房間。

A How are you going?
你好嗎？

B I wanna get away from here.
我想要逃離這裡。

A What's your plan?
你的計畫是什麼？

B I wanna take them to the zoo.
我想要帶他們去動物園。

A I wanna change my hair.
我想要改變我的髮型。

B You don't have to. You look great.
你不需要。你看起來很棒！

I always get up at 7 A.M.
我總是在早上七點起床。

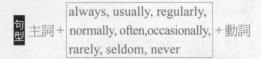

句型 主詞 + always, usually, regularly, normally, often, occasionally, rarely, seldom, never + 動詞

A When do you do your homework?
你什麼時候做你的功課？

B I often do my homework after dinner.
我通常在晚餐後做我的功課。

A Does David usually play football?
大衛經常踢足球嗎？

B Yes, he usually plays football.
是的，他經常踢足球。

A He will never go there again.
他再也不會去那裡了。

B What's the matter with him?
他發生什麼事了？

A She rarely visits her aunt.
她難得去看望她的阿姨。

B I thought they were close.
我以為他們很親近。

A She seldom showed her feelings.
她很少表露感情。

B What happened to her?
她發生什麼事了？

How many brothers do you have?

你有幾個兄弟？

句型 many + 可數名詞複數

A How many brothers do you have?
你有幾個兄弟？

B I have two brothers.
我有兩個兄弟。

A How many classes does Marla have today?
瑪莉亞今天有多少堂課？

B She has three classes today.
她今天有三堂課。

A How many candies do you eat?
你吃多少巧克力？

B I eat two bars of chocolate every day.
我每天吃兩條巧克力。

A How many letters does she write every day?
她每天寫多少封信？

B She writes two letters every day.
她每天寫兩封信。

A How many countries are there in the world?
世界上有多少國家？

B I don't know.
我不知道。

How much is it?

這個賣多少錢？

句型 much + 不可數名詞

A Where is your money?
你的錢到哪裡去了？

B I don't earn much money.
我沒有賺很多錢。

A How much sugar do you take in your coffee?
你要在咖啡裡加多少糖？

B One teaspoon, please.
請給我一茶匙。

A How much rent do you pay?
你付多少租金？

B I pay five thousand dollars.
我付五千元。

A There's so much music that takes place in Taipei.
在台北有很多音樂產生。

B Great. I'm glad to hear that.
很好。我很高興聽見這件事。

A There is so much fun in this kind of party.
這類派對上有很多好玩的事。

B Not for me.
對我來説不算是。

A There is so much wrong with it.
有好多錯誤。

B What's matter with it?
發生什麼事？

I am in charge of it.
由我負責。

 句型 be 動詞 + in charge (of + 某事)

A Who is in charge now?
現在是誰負責？

B I am in charge of it.
由我負責。

A Who is in charge of this?
誰負責這件事？

B I am.
是我。

A Who is in charge of my privacy?
誰負責我的隱私？

B It's Mr. Smith.
是史密斯先生。

A Who is in charge of this plan?
是誰負責這個計畫的？

B I don't know.
我不知道。

A Who is in charge of Russia Policy?
誰負責俄羅斯的政策？

B It's Minister of Defence.
是國防部長。

A I'm in charge of this project.
我負責這個計畫。

B I am David White. And you are?
我是大衛·懷特。你是？

Get in touch with us.

要和我們保持聯絡。

句型 get in touch with + 某人

A Please get in touch with us.
請和我們保持聯絡。

B I will.
我會的。

A Did you get in touch with David?
你有和大衛保持聯絡嗎？

B Yes, I did.
是的，我有。

A You can get in touch with him in the following days.
接下來的日子你可以和他保持聯絡。

B OK. What's his telephone number?
好的。他的電話號碼是幾號？

A You may get in touch with David.
你可以和大衛保持聯絡。

B Why should I get in touch with him?
為什麼我要和他保持聯絡？

A I'll get in touch with my coach.
我會和我的教練保持聯絡。

B Are you sure?
你確定嗎？

A Have you seen Maria?
你有看見瑪莉亞嗎？

B Yes, I did get in touch with her.
是的，我有和她保持聯絡。

There's something weird.

事情很詭異！

句型 there is something + 形容詞 / 子句

A There's something weird.
事情很詭異。

B I don't think so.
我不這麼認為。

A There's something strange.
事有蹊蹺。

B How come? What happen?
為什麼？發生什麼事？

A There's something different.
事情變得不一樣。

B What kind of difference?
有什麼不同？

A Are you OK? You look terrible.
你還好吧？你看起來糟透了。

B There's something wrong with me.
我不太對勁。

A What happened to Maria?
瑪莉亞怎麼了？

B There's something I don't know about her.
我不太知道她的一些事。

A There's something I'd like to show you.
我要給你看一些東西。

B What? What is it?
什麼？什麼事？

I feel like studying.
我想要唸書。

句型 feel like + 動名詞

A	I feel like studying. 我想要唸書。
B	Of course. Go ahead. 當然好。去吧！
A	I feel like taking a walk. 我想要散步。
B	OK. Let's go. 好啊！我們走。
A	I feel like taking a shower. 我想要沖個澡。
B	You really should. 你真的應該。
A	I feel like having dinner with my family. 我想要和我的家人共進晚餐。
B	It's good for you. 對你來說是好的。
A	I feel like changing the color of it. 我想要改變它的顏色。
B	What color do you want? 你想要什麼顏色？
A	I feel like going to the USA. 我想要去美國。
B	Are you going to visit your family? 你要去探望你的家人嗎？

Forgive me, but you are wrong.

原諒我的指責,但是你錯了。

句型 Forgive me, but + 子句

A Forgive me, but you are wrong.
原諒我,但是你是錯的。

B **You really think so?**
你真的這麼認為?

A Forgive me, but I'd better get going.
原諒我,但是我應該要走了。

B **Sure. Please say hi to David for me.**
好啊!請幫我向大衛問候。

A Forgive me, but I don't want to join you.
原諒我,但是我不想加入你(們)。

B **It's all right.**
沒關係。

A Forgive me, but I don't agree with you.
原諒我,但是我不同意你。

B **What is your opinion?**
你的意見是什麼?

A Forgive me, but what do you mean by that?
原諒我,但是你是什麼意思?

B **I mean we should try to avoid it.**
我的意思是我們應該要試著避免。

Let's do it all day long.

我們一整天都這麼做吧！

句型 主詞 + 動詞 + all day long

A Let's do it all day long.
我們一整天都這麼做吧！

B It's a good idea.
好主意。

A I could listen to this all day long.
我可以一整天都聽這個。

B Are you crazy? All day long?
你瘋啦？一整天？

A You can watch TV all day long.
你可以一整天看電視。

B Are you serious?
你是說真的嗎？

A I thought about it all day long.
我一整天都在思考這件事。

B And what's your decision?
那你的決定是什麼？

A I played the baseball all day long.
我一整天都在打棒球。

B Good for you.
對你來說很好。

A We were chatting all day long.
我們聊了一整天了。

B What were you chatting about?
你們聊了些什麼？

I get very sick.

我病得很重。

句型 get + 過去分詞 / 形容詞

A You look terrible. Are you OK?
你看起來糟透了。你還好吧？

B I get very sick.
我病得很重。

A I get very wet.
我很濕。

B What happen to you?
你怎麼啦？

A I get very tired.
我很累。

B You should get some sleep.
你應該要睡一下覺。

A I get very mad.
我很瘋狂。

B Don't be so mad, OK?
不要這麼瘋狂，好嗎？

A I get very nervous.
我很緊張。

B Don't worry about it.
不用擔心。

A How is the weather?
天氣怎麼樣？

B It's getting cold.
天氣越來越冷。

I'd better get going.
我最好離開。

句型 had better + 原形動詞

A I'd better get going.
我最好離開。

B OK. See you next week.
好。下週見。

A I'd better talk to David.
我最好和大衛談談。

B OK. I'll get him.
好。我去叫他來。

A I'd better give him a call.
我最好打電話給他。

B What are you trying to say?
你想要說什麼？

A I'd better get him out.
我最好救他出來。

B He is not your responsibility.
他不是你的責任。

A I'd better leave him alone.
我最好不要管他。

B And don't try to change his mind.
而且不要試著去改變他的決定。

A I'd better forget everything.
我最好忘記所有的事。

B How could you do that?
你怎麼可以這麼做？

I'd rather give up.

我寧願放棄。

句型 would rather + 原形動詞 + (than + 原形動詞)

A I'd rather give up.
我寧願放棄。

B You should stop thinking about that.
你應該停止這麼想。

A I'd rather hang out with David.
我寧願和大衛在一起。

D David? I don't think so.
大衛？我不這麼認為。

A I'd rather turn on the light.
我寧願打開燈。

B It's not so dark, OK?
沒這麼黑，好嗎？

A I'd rather eat a hot dog.
我寧願吃熱狗。

B But I want to have French fries.
但是我想要吃薯條。

A I'd rather pay higher taxes.
我寧願付高一點的稅金。

B Are you an idiot?
你是白癡嗎？

A I'd rather go for a walk than watch TV.
我寧願去散步也不要看電視。

B Go ahead. It's good for you.
去吧！對你來說很好。

I'd finish it first.

我會先完成。

句型 would +原形動詞~ + first

A
I'd finish it first.
我會先完成。

B
No problem. It's up to you.
沒問題。由你自己決定。

A
I'd kill myself first.
我會先殺了我自己。

B
Don't say that. It's not your fault.
不要這麼說。這不是你的錯。

A
I'd call Mr. Smith first.
我會先打電話給史密斯先生。

B
No, I don't think so. Try to contact Mr. White first.
不，我不這麼認為。試著先聯絡懷特先生。

A
I'd go for a walk first.
我會先去散步。

B
Let me go with you.
我和你去。

A
I'd make a wish first.
我會先許願。

B
Sure. What would you wish?
可以。你會許什麼願望？

A
I'd type this letter first.
我會先打這封信。

B
Good. Send it to me when you finish it.
很好。完成後寄給我。

Tell me what you think.

告訴我你想什麼。

句型 tell someone + | wh- 子句 |
| how 子句 |

A Tell me what your name is.
你可以告訴我你的名字。

B My name is David White.
我的名字是大衛·懷特。

A Tell me what time it is now.
告訴我現在足幾點鐘。

B It's ten to five.
現在差十分就五點。

A Tell me what they said.
告訴我他們說了什麼。

B They said you are their son.
他們說你是他們的兒子。

A Tell me what you want.
告訴我你想要什麼。

B You tell me.
你告訴我啊！

A Tell me what color you like.
告訴我你喜歡什麼顏色。

B It's black.
是黑色。

Tell me how to use it.

告訴我如何使用。

句型 tell someone + $\dfrac{\text{wh-}}{\text{how}}$ + to + 原形動詞

A Can you tell me where to get?
你能告訴我要去哪裡嗎？

B Sure. Just go straight ahead.
好啊！只要直走就可以。

A Can you tell me how to use it?
你能告訴我如何使用嗎？

B OK. See? It's not difficult.
好的。看見了嗎？不難的。

A Can you tell me how to pronounce it?
你能告訴我如何發音嗎？

B No problem. Watch my mouth.
沒問題。看著我的嘴巴！

A Can you tell me how to repair it?
你能告訴我如何修理嗎？

B Let's see.
我來看看。

A Can you tell me how to do it?
你能告訴我如何做嗎？

B Sorry, I am not familiar with it.
抱歉，我不太熟悉這個。

A Can you tell me what to say?
你能告訴我要說什麼嗎？

B Sorry, I don't know, either.
抱歉，我也不知道。

You know what I'm saying?

你明白我說什麼嗎？

句型	know understand	+	wh- 子句 how 子句

A You know what I'm saying?
你明白我說的嗎？

B Excuse me?
你說什麼？

A I don't know what you mean.
我不知道你是什麼意思。

B I mean he is the best one for this job.
我的意思是他是這個職位的最佳人選。

A I don't know where David was off to.
我不知道大衛去哪裡了。

B I saw him leaving the house.
我看到他離開房子了。

A He didn't know what I was trying to say.
他不知道我想要說什麼。

B What did you react?
你有什麼反應？

A I don't understand how you do it.
我不瞭解你如何辦到的。

B I'll let you know.
我會讓你知道的。

A We don't understand how you finished it.
我們不瞭解你是如何完成的。

B This is a secret.
這是秘密。

What a perfect example.

真是一個絕佳的典範。

句型 what + 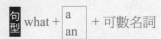 a an + 可數名詞

A What a perfect example.
真是一個絕佳的典範。

B You really think so?
你真的這樣認為嗎？

A Wow, what a wonderful place.
哇，好棒的地方。

B We will camp here for the night.
我們會在這裡搭營過夜。

A David? What are you doing here?
大衛？你在這裡做什麼？

B Hi. What a coincidence.
嗨！真是巧合！

A What an idiot.
真是笨蛋一個！

B I beg your pardon?
你説什麼？

A What an adorable kid.
真是一個可愛的孩子。

B Thanks.
謝謝！

You are such a sweetie.

你真是個小甜心。

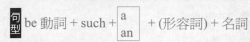

句型 be 動詞 + such + | a / an | + (形容詞) + 名詞

A Come on. Let me help you with it.
來吧！我來幫你！

B You are such a sweetie.
你真是個小甜心。

A You are such a jerk.
你真是混蛋！

B Excuse me?
你說什麼？

A You are such a man.
你真是個男人！

B Yeah? Am I?
是嗎？我是嗎？

A He is such a little devil.
他真是個小惡魔！

B Yeah. He is only 18 months old.
是啊！他才一歲半而已啊！

A She is such an angle.
她真是個小天使。

B That's right.
沒錯！

A Maria is such an amazing actress.
瑪莉亞是一位很棒的演員。

B She is my favorite actress.
她是我最喜歡的女演員。

Anything wrong?

有問題嗎？

句型 | anything
     | something | ＋形容詞

A Anything wrong?
有問題嗎？

B Yes, I'd like to talk with you.
是的，我想要和你談一談。

A Is there anything wrong?
有問題嗎？

B No. Everything is fine.
沒有。每件事都很好。

A Anything new?
有什麼新鮮事嗎？

B Haven't you heard of it?
你沒聽說這件事嗎？

A Can't you hear that?
你沒有聽見嗎？

B What? Something wrong?
什麼？有問題嗎？

A It sounds something awful.
這事聽起來真是可怕。

B I know. But I have tried my best.
我知道。但是我已經盡力了。

A Don't you think something different?
你不覺得事情不太一樣嗎？

B I don't think so.
我不這麼認為。

I'm crazy about her.
我很喜歡她。

 句型　be 動詞 + crazy about + 某人 / 某事

A How do you like her?
你覺得她如何？

B I'm crazy about her.
我很喜歡她。

A Is David falling in love?
大衛有陷入愛河中嗎？

B Yes. David is crazy about Maria.
是的。大衛瘋狂地愛上了瑪莉亞。

A Do you love David?
你愛大衛嗎？

B Yes. I'm crazy about this guy.
有啊！我瘋狂愛上這傢伙！

A Are you seeing someone?
你有和誰在交往中嗎？

B I love one girl. I am crazy about her.
我喜歡一個女孩。我為她瘋狂。

A Do you like American movies?
你喜歡美國電影嗎？

B I'm crazy about American movies.
我瘋狂喜歡美國電影。

A What do you do for fun?
你有什麼興趣？

B I'm crazy about football.
我瘋迷足球。

Be quiet.
安靜點！

 句型 be 動詞 + 形容詞 / a, an + 形容詞 + 名詞

A Be quiet.
安靜點！

B Sorry.
抱歉！

A Be good.
要乖！

B I will.
我會的。

A Be patient.
要有耐心！

B But I just don't want to do it.
但是我就是不想去做這件事。

A Be a good boy.
要當一個好男孩！

B OK. I will be a good boy.
好的。我會當一個好

A Be a polite gentleman.
要當個有禮貌的紳士。

B It's not my style.
我不是這一型的。

A Don't be an idiot.
不要當一個混蛋！

B I beg your pardon?
你說什麼？

May I help you?
需要我幫助嗎？

句型 help + 某人

A May I help you?
需要我幫助嗎？

B Yes, I'd like to check in.
是的，我要辦理報到。

A May I help you?
需要我幫助嗎？

B Yes. I don't know where I am
是的，我不知道自己身在何處。

A May I help you?
需要我幫助嗎？

D Yes. Where is the theater?
是的。戲院在哪裡？

A May I help you?
需要我幫助嗎？

B May I have some more bread?
我可以再多要一些麵包嗎？

A May I help you?
需要我幫助嗎？

B Thanks. Where is the restroom?
謝謝！洗手間在哪裡？

A May I help you?
需要我幫助嗎？

B No. I can handle it.
不用。我可以自己處理。

I will.

我會的。/我願意。

句型 主詞 + will + (原形動詞)

A Try harder, OK?
努力一點，好嗎？

B I will.
我會的。

A Be there on time.
要準時到達那裡。

B Don't worry about it. I will.
不用擔心。我會的。

A Will you come along?
你會一起來嗎？

B Yes, I will.
是的，我會的。

A Will you let me leave?
你會讓我離開嗎？

B Of course, I will.
當然啦！我會的。

A You will call me, won't you?
你會打電話給我吧？對嗎？

B Yes, I will.
是的，我會的。

A Will you lend me your book?
你會把你的書借給我嗎？

B No, I won't.
不，我不會的。

Are you sure?

你確定？

 be 動詞 + sure (+ about)

A I'm going to his birthday party.
我要去參加他的生日派對。

B Are you sure?
你確定？

A I have decided to quit.
我已經決定要辭職。

B Are you sure?
你確定？

A I don't want to play baseball.
我不想要打棒球。

B Are you sure?
你確定？

A Could I exchange this one?
我可以換掉這個嗎？

B Are you sure?
你確定？

A Can I go swimming with David?
我可以和大衛去游泳嗎？

B Are you sure?
你確定？

A What's wrong with him?
他怎麼啦？

B I'm not really sure.
我不是很確定。

I'm starving.

我餓壞了。

句型 be 動詞 + 動名詞

A I'm starving.
我餓壞了。

B Let's get something to eat.
我們吃點東西吧！

A Hello? Anybody home?
哈囉？有人在家嗎？

B I am coming.
我來了。

A What are you doing?
你在做什麼？

B I am painting my bathroom.
我在油漆我的房間。

A What are you doing?
你在做什麼？

B I am doing my homework.
我在做我的功課。

A Are you busy now?
你現在在忙嗎？

B Yes, I am cooking dinner.
是的，我在煮晚餐。

A Where are you off to?
你要去哪裡？

B I'm fixing to go to the cinema now.
我現在要去戲院。

Part

6

道地俚語

Don't make a fool of me.
不要愚弄我！

A Check it out.
你看看！

B Don't make a fool of me.
不要愚弄我！

A Come over here.
過來這裡！

B Don't make a fool of me.
不要愚弄我！

A Do you want it back?
來拿啊！

B Don't make a fool of me.
不要愚弄我！

A Take a look.
你看！

B Don't make a fool of me.
不要愚弄我！

A Did you see that?
你有看見了那個嗎？

B Don't make a fool of me.
不要愚弄我！

A It's no big deal.
這沒什麼！

B Don't make a fool of me.
不要愚弄我！

I am fed up with it.
我厭煩死了！

A What happened?
發生什麼事啦？

B I am fed up with it.
我厭煩死了！

A Are you OK?
你還好吧？

B I was fed up with my boss.
我對我的老闆煩透了。

A You look upset.
你看起來很沮喪喔！

B I am fed up with it.
我厭煩死了！

A I am fed up with it.
我厭煩死了！

B Come on. Cheer up.
不要這樣！高興點！

相關用法

I have had enough!
我真是受夠了！

A I have had enough!
我真是受夠了！

B Why? What did he do?
為什麼？他做了什麼事？

Let's call it a day.

今天到這裡就結束吧!

A It's already 10 P.M.
已經晚上十點了。

B Let's call it a day.
今天到這裡就結束吧!

A It's pretty late now.
現在很晚了!

B Let's call it a day.
今天到這裡就結束吧!

A We should go home now.
我們現在應該要回家。

B Let's call it a day.
今天到這裡就結束吧!

A Let's call it a day.
今天到這裡就結束吧!

B Great. Let's get out of here.
太好了!我們離開這裡吧!

A Let's call it a day.
今天到這裡就結束吧!

B Great. I'm so exhausted.
太好了!我好累!

A Let's call it a day.
今天到這裡就結束吧!

B All right! I'm starving.
好啊!我好餓!

I fall in love with David.
我愛上了大衛。

A Did you fall in love with that guy?
你愛上那傢伙了？

B Yes, I fall in love with David.
是的，我愛上大衛。

A Are you seeing someone now?
你現在有交往的對象嗎？

B It's David. I fall in love with him.
是大衛。我愛上他了。

A Something wrong?
怎麼啦？

B Well, I fall in love with Maria.
嗯…我愛上瑪莉亞。

A What happened?
發生什事？

B I fall in love with him.
我愛上他。

A I fall in love with her.
我愛上她。

B Oh, my God. Really?
喔！天啊！真的嗎？

A What's going on between David and you?
你和大衛之間怎麼了？

B I fall in love with him.
我愛上他。

You mess it up.

你弄得亂七八糟！

A Look. You mess it up.
看！你弄得亂七八糟！

B Not me.
不是我。

A Look. You mess it up.
看！你弄得亂七八糟！

B I didn't do it.
我沒做。

A Look. You mess it up.
看！你弄得亂七八糟！

B It's David.
是大衛！

A Look. You mess it up.
看！你弄得亂七八糟！

B I'm so sorry.
我很抱歉。

A Look. You mess it up.
看！你弄得亂七八糟！

B Please forgive me.
請原諒我！

A Look. You mess it up.
看！你弄得亂七八糟！

B I won't do it again.
我不會再做了！

You screw it up.

你搞砸了！

A You screw it up.
你搞砸了！

B I am so sorry.
我很抱歉。

A You screw it up.
你搞砸了！

B I can't help it
我無能為力。

A You screw it up.
你搞砸了！

B I don't think so.
我不應認為。

A You screw it up.
你搞砸了！

B What makes you think so?
你為什麼會這麼認為？

A You screw it up.
你搞砸了！

B How could you say that?
你怎麼能這麼說？

A You screw it up.
你搞砸了！

B But it's not my fault.
但是這不是我的錯。

Shall we?

要走了嗎？

A Shall we?
要走了嗎？

B Sure, let's go.
好啊！走吧！

A Shall we?
要走了嗎？

B I'm not ready.
我還沒準備好。

A Shall we?
要走了嗎？

B No. One more thing.
沒有。還有一件事。

A Shall we?
要走了嗎？

B Wait a moment.
等一下。

A Shall we?
要走了嗎？

B I'll catch you up.
我會趕上你。

A Shall we?
要走了嗎？

B I don't think so.
我不這麼認為。

How about that?

那個如何？

A How about that?
那個如何？

B I don't like it.
我不喜歡它。

A How about that?
那個如何？

B I don't think so.
我不這麼認為。

A How about that?
那個如何？

B Great, I guess.
我猜很好吧！

A How about that?
那個如何？

B Not bad.
不錯。

A How about that?
那個如何？

B What do you think?
你覺得呢？

A How about that?
那個如何？

B Maybe it's a good idea.
可能是個好主意。

How are you?

你好嗎?

A	How are you? 你好嗎?
B	**Great.** 很好!
A	How are you? 你好嗎?
B	**Terrific.** 不錯。
A	How are you? 你好嗎?
B	**Never better.** 再好不過了。
A	How are you? 你好嗎?
B	**Pretty good. And you?** 很好!你呢?
A	How are you? 你好嗎?
B	**So-so.** 馬馬虎虎。
A	How are you? 你好嗎?
B	**Not so good.** 不太好。

Something wrong?

有問題嗎？

A Something wrong?
有問題嗎？

B Yes, I had a car accident yesterday.
是的，我昨天發生了車禍。

A Something wrong?
有問題嗎？

B Yes, I need to talk with you.
是的，我需要和你談一談。

A Something wrong?
有問題嗎？

B I need your help.
我需要你的幫助。

A Something wrong?
有問題嗎？

B I saw a strange man the other day.
前幾天我看見一個陌生人。

A Something wrong?
有問題嗎？

B No. Everything is fine.
沒事。一切都很好。

A Something wrong?
有問題嗎？

B No. Not at all.
沒事。完全沒事。

I am serious.

我是認真的。

| A | **Are you joking?**
你開玩笑的吧？ |
| B | I am serious.
我是認真的。 |

| A | **You meant it?**
你是當真的？ |
| B | I am serious.
我是認真的。 |

| A | **I don't buy it.**
我不相信。 |
| B | I am serious.
我是認真的。 |

| A | **It's impossible.**
不可能的。 |
| B | I am serious.
我是認真的。 |

| A | **Are you crazy?**
你瘋啦？ |
| B | I am serious.
我是認真的。 |

| A | **You'll be sorry.**
你會後悔的。 |
| B | I am serious.
我是認真的。 |

I know how you feel.
我瞭解你的感受。

A Thank you for being with me.
謝謝你陪我！

B I know how you feel.
我瞭解你的感受。

A Thank you for everything.
凡事謝啦！

B I know how you feel.
我瞭解你的感受。

A Thank you for all these.
這一切都要謝謝你！

B I know how you feel.
我瞭解你的感受。

A Thank you for what you have done.
謝謝你所做的一切。

B I know how you feel.
我瞭解你的感受。

A Just leave me alone.
不要管我！

B I know how you feel.
我瞭解你的感受。

A I don't know what else I can do.
我不知道我還能做什麼。

B I know how you feel.
我瞭解你的感受。

No more excuses.

不要再找藉口了。

A	Listen to me, please. 請聽我説。
B	No more excuses. 不要再找藉口了。

A	Shut up. 閉嘴！
B	No more excuses. 不要再找藉口了。

A	I don't want to hear it. 我不想聽。
B	No more excuses. 不要再找藉口了。

A	I am innocent. 我是無辜的。
B	No more excuses. 不要再找藉口了。

A	It's not my fault. 這不是我的錯。
B	No more excuses. 不要再找藉口了。

A	It's not truth. 這不是事實。
B	No more excuses. 不要再找藉口了。

Say no more.

不要再說了！

A Listen to me.
聽我說！

B Say no more.
不要再說了！

A You are not listening.
你沒在聽。

B Say no more.
不要再說了！

A You are not listening to me.
你沒在聽我說。

B Say no more.
不要再說了！

A Do you hear me?
你有聽到我(說的)嗎？

B Say no more.
不要再說了！

A It's your fault.
這是你的錯！

B Say no more.
不要再說了！

A What do you want me to say?
你要我說什麼？

B Say no more.
不要再說了！

Say something.

說點話吧！(有什麼意見？)

A Say something.
說點話吧！

B What do you want me to say?
你想要我說什麼？

A Say something.
說點話吧！

B I have no idea.
我不知道。

A Say something.
說點話吧！

B Well, I will figure it out.
嗯，我會算出來。

A Say something.
說點話吧！

B I will see what I can do.
我來看看我能做什麼。

A Say something.
說點話吧！

B I do what I do.
我會盡量。

A Say something.
說點話吧！

B Relax. I have an idea.
放輕鬆點！我有個主意。

Believe it or not.

隨你相不相信！

A Are you sure about it?
你確定？

B Believe it or not.
隨你相不相信！

A Get out of here.
少來了！

B Believe it or not.
隨你相不相信！

A Are you kidding me?
你開玩笑吧？

B Believe it or not.
隨你相不相信！

A I don't know. It seems so odd.
我不知道。似乎很奇怪。

B Believe it or not.
隨你相不相信！

A How old is she?
她多大年紀？

B Believe it or not, she's only 4 years old!
隨你相不相信，她只有四歲。

A What do you think of it?
你覺得呢？

B I like this one, believe it or not.
隨你相不相信，我喜歡這一個。

Anything doing?

有什麼活動嗎？有什麼事嗎？辦得到嗎？

A Anything doing tonight?
今晚有什麼活動嗎？

B Yeah, we're going to a concert.
有啊，我們要去聽演唱會。

A Anything doing tonight?
今晚有什麼活動嗎？

B We will go shopping.
我們會去逛街。

A Anything doing tonight?
今晚有什麼活動嗎？

B Wanna see a movie with me?
要和我去看電影嗎？

A Anything doing tonight?
今晚有什麼活動嗎？

B Nope. Nothing.
沒事！沒啥事！

A Anything doing tonight?
今晚有什麼活動嗎？

B What do you say?
你有什麼建議嗎？

A Anything doing tonight?
今晚有什麼活動嗎？

B Why? Do you have any plans?
為什麼(這麼問)？你有什麼計畫嗎？

What's new?

最近怎麼樣？

A What's new?
最近怎麼樣？

B Nothing special.
沒什麼特別的。

A What's new?
最近怎麼樣？

B So far so good.
目前為止都還好。

A What's new?
最近怎麼樣？

B Not so good.
不太好。

A What's new?
最近怎麼樣？

B Terrible.
糟透了！

A What's new?
最近怎麼樣？

B Everything is fine.
都還不錯。

A What's new?
最近怎麼樣？

B Still the same.
老樣子。

It's a deal.

就這麼說定了。

A Why don't we leave now?
我們何不現在就離開？

B OK, it's a deal.
好，就這麼說定了。

A Two thousand for these two coats?
這兩件外套算兩千？

B OK, it's a deal.
好，就這麼說定了。

A I'll pick you up tomorrow morning.
我明天早上會來接你。

B OK, it's a deal.
好，就這麼說定了。

A I promise, OK?
我保證，好嗎？

B OK, it's a deal.
好，就這麼說定了。

A Let's have a get-together.
我們應該要聚一聚。

B OK, it's a deal.
好，就這麼說定了。

A I'll call her for you.
我會幫你打電話給她。

B OK, it's a deal.
好，就這麼說定了。

Hello. Stranger.

好久不見啦！(遇見久未見面的熟人)

A Hello. Stranger.
好久不見啦！

B David?
大衛？

A Hello. Stranger.
好久不見啦！

B Hi, David.
嗨，大衛！

A Hello. Stranger.
好久不見啦！

B David? Is that you?
大衛？是你嗎？

A Hello. Stranger.
好久不見啦！

B David? What are you doing here?
大衛？你在這裡做什麼？

A Hello. Stranger.
好久不見啦！

B Hey, good to see you again.
嘿，很高興又見到你。

A Hello. Stranger.
好久不見啦！

B Hey, long time no see.
嘿，好久不見。

That's news to me.
我沒聽說過。

A I don't know if that's true.
我不知道是否是事實。

B That's news to me.
我沒聽說過。

A Don't you think so?
你不這麼認為嗎？

B Well, that's news to me.
嗯，我沒聽說過。

A You don't know about it?
你不知道？

B Wow, that's news to me.
哇，我沒聽說過。

A I've decided to quit.
我已經決定要辭職了。

B OK, that's news to me.
是喔，我沒聽說過。

A I broke up with Maria.
我和瑪莉亞分手了。

B Really? That's news to me.
真的？我沒聽說過。

A David was sentenced to death.
大衛被判死刑了。

B Oh, my God. That's news to me.
喔，我的天啊！我沒聽說過。

What the hell?

搞什麼？

A Check it out.
看！

B What the hell?
搞什麼？

A Did you see that?
你有看見那個嗎？

B What the hell is that?
那是什麼東西？

A I'll show you this.
我會給你看這個東西。

B What the hell is this?
這是什麼東西？

A What a mess.
真是亂七八糟。

B What the hell is going on here?
這裡發生什麼事？

A David? Is that you?
大衛？是你嗎？

B What the hell are you doing here?
你在這裡做什麼？

A Someone tell me where David is?
有誰要告訴我大衛在哪裡？

B What the hell happened to David?
大衛發生什麼事了？

I'll see.

再說吧！

A Can I have another cake?
我可以再要一片餅乾嗎？

B I'll see.
再說吧！

A I don't want to go to school.
我不想要去學校。

B I'll see.
再說吧！

A Can I spend the night over there?
我可以在那裡過夜嗎？

B I'll see.
再說吧！

A Can Maria stay the night?
瑪莉亞可以留下來過夜嗎？

B I'll see.
再說吧！

相關用法

We'll see.

再說吧！

A Are we going to stay here?
我們要停留在這裡嗎？

B We'll see.
再說吧！

I'll meet you there.

我會在那裡等你。

A I'll meet you there.
我會在那裡等你。

B OK. See you.
好！再見！

A I'll meet you there.
我會在那裡等你。

B Sure. Catch you later.
好！晚點見！

A I'll meet you there.
我會在那裡等你。

B Bye.
再見！

A Shall we say about ten o'clock?
我們約 10 點如何？

B I'll meet you there.
我會在那裡等你。

相關用法

I'll see you there.

我會在那裡等你。

A I'll see you there.
我會在那裡等你。

B Sure. Be there on time.
好。要準時到喔！

I am impressed.
我印象深刻。

A What do you think?
你覺得呢？

B I am impressed.
我印象深刻。

A What's your opinion?
你的意見是什麼？

B I am impressed.
我印象深刻。

A How do you like it?
你喜歡嗎？

B I am impressed.
我印象深刻。

A Isn't it cool?
很酷吧！

B I am impressed.
我印象深刻。

A Do you believe that?
你相信嗎？

B I am impressed.
我印象深刻。

A See? I've told you so.
看吧！我就告訴過你了。

B Yeah, I am impressed.
是啊！我印象深刻。

You don't say?

真的嗎?(不會是這樣吧!)

A	I saw a huge dinosaur. 我看見了一隻大恐龍。
B	You don't say? 真的嗎?
A	I went to see a movie with Maria. 我和瑪莉亞去看電影了。
B	You don't say? 真的嗎?
A	I won't give him another chance. 我不會再給他另一次機會。
B	You don't say? 真的嗎?
A	I didn't ask him to stay with me. 我沒有要求他留下來陪我。
B	You don't say? 真的嗎?
A	There are so many spiders in my room. 我房間裡有好多蜘蛛。
B	You don't say? 真的嗎?
A	He asked me to have dinner with him. 他要求我和他一起吃晚餐。
B	You don't say? 真的嗎?

You could say that.

我同意你的看法。

A I planned to finish it on this Friday.
我計劃好了這個星期五要去釣魚。

B You could say that.
我同意你的看法。

A I won't let it happen again.
我不會再讓這件事發生。

B You could say that.
我同意你的看法。

A The train would come in early, I guess.
我猜火車會很早到達。

B You could say that.
我同意你的看法。

A We don't need to buy a new carpet.
我們不需要買條新地毯。

B You could say that.
我同意你的看法。

A We better get going!
我們最好馬上就走！

B You could say that.
我同意你的看法。

A Why don't we just pick her up?
我們何不就去接她？

B You could say that.
我同意你的看法。

Let's change the subject.

我們換個話題吧！

A Why don't you apologize to her?
你為什麼不向她道歉？

B Let's change the subject.
我們換個話題吧！

A You don't deserve her.
你配不上她。

B Let's change the subject.
我們換個話題吧！

A IIow could you do that?
你怎麼可以這麼做？

B Let's change the subject.
我們換個話題吧！

A Don't you think you made a mistake?
你不覺得你犯錯了嗎？

B Let's change the subject.
我們換個話題吧！

A You failed the math exam, right?
你沒考好數學考試，對吧？

B Let's change the subject.
我們換個話題吧！

A Talk about your family.
聊一聊你的家人吧！

B Let's change the subject.
我們換個話題吧！

Suit yourself.

隨便你！

A I want to hang out with Maria.
我想要和瑪莉亞在一起。

B Suit yourself.
隨便你！

A I don't want to be there.
我不要過去。

B Suit yourself.
隨便你！

A I don't need your help.
我不需要你的幫忙。

B Suit yourself.
隨便你！

相關用法

Whatever.

隨便你。

A Maybe I could go shopping.
也許我可以去逛街。

B Whatever. Just leave me alone.
隨便你。不要管我。

A How about fishing with David?
要不要和大衛去釣魚？

B Whatever.
隨便你。

I don't mind.

我不在意。

A How about your dreams?
你的夢想麼辦？

B I don't mind.
我不在意。

A Don't you want to complete it on time?
你不想要準時完成嗎？

B I don't mind.
我不在意。

A It's your responsibility
這是你的責任。

B I don't mind.
我不在意。

相關用法

I don't give a shit!

我不在乎。

A You don't love him anymore?
你不再愛他了嗎？

B I don't give a shit!
我不在乎。

A But she is your younger sister.
但是她是你妹妹啊！

B I don't give a shit.
我不在乎。

I suppose so.
我猜是如此！

A	I think David is a loser. 我覺得大衛是個失敗者。
B	I suppose so. 我猜是如此！
A	Is Maria seeing someone else? 瑪莉亞有交往的對象嗎？
B	I suppose so. 我猜是如此！
A	David didn't want this job, either. 大衛也不想要這個工作。
B	I suppose so. 我猜是如此！
A	She refused your offer, right? 她拒絕你的提議，對吧？
B	I suppose so. 我猜是如此！
A	Did you go to the same school? 你們以前是同校學生嗎？
B	I suppose so. 我猜是如此！
A	Did your parents get a divorce? 你的父母離婚了嗎？
B	I suppose so. 我猜是如此！

Now you're talking.

這才像話。(你說得對極了！)

A I decided to go back with David.
我決定要和大衛一起回去了。

B Now you're talking.
這才像話。

A I won't let her leave me again.
我不會再讓她離開我。

B Now you're talking.
這才像話。

A I think we should come over.
我覺得我們應該要過去。

B Now you're talking.
你說得對極了！

A It's my job.
這是我的工作。

B Now you're talking.
這才像話。

A Let's have dinner some other day.
改天一起吃個晚餐吧！

B Now you're talking.
這才像話。

A Isn't that possible?
沒有可能嗎？

B Now you're talking.
你說得對極了！

I'm not telling.

我不會說的。

A What's your opinion?
你的意見是什麼？

B I'm not telling.
我不會說的。

A What do you think about it?
你覺得呢？

B I'm not telling.
我不會說的。

A What would you tell us?
你要告訴我們什麼事？

B I'm not telling.
我不會說的。

A Do you have anything to say?
你有什麼話要說嗎？

B I'm not telling.
我不會說的。

A Do you have any ideas about it?
你有什意見嗎？

B I'm not telling.
我不會說的。

A What's the truth?
真相是什麼？

B I'm not telling.
我不會說的。

I need to talk with you.

我需要和你談一談。

A I need to talk with you.
我需要和你談一談。

B Sure. Have a seat.
好啊！請坐！

A I need to talk with you.
我需要和你談一談。

B What can I help you?
需要我幫什麼忙？

A I need to talk with you.
我需要和你談一談。

B What's up?
什麼事？

A I need to talk with you.
我需要和你談一談。

B But I'm busy now.
可是我現在很忙。

相關用法

Can I talk to you now?

我現在可以和你談一談嗎？

A Can I talk to you now?
我現在可以和你談一談嗎？

B Sure. What is it?
當然可以！(怎麼啦？)

Try me.

說來聽聽。可以試試看。

A You are not gonna believe it.
你一定不相信。

B Try me.
說來聽聽。

A You are not my style.
你不是我喜歡的類型。

B Try me.
可以試試看啊！

A You can't do this.
你辦不到。

B Try me.
可以試試看。

A I'll kill you.
我要殺了你。

B Try me.
試試看你敢不敢。

A I won't let you go.
我不會讓你離開。

B Try me.
要不要試試看。

A I don't trust you.
我不相信你。

B Try me.
可以試試看。

You're not listening to me.

你沒聽我說話。你沒有聽我的話去做。

A What did you just say?
你剛剛說什麼？

B You're not listening to me.
你沒聽我說話。

A What happen?
發生什麼事？

B You're not listening to me.
你沒聽我說話。

A What about now?
現在怎麼樣？

B You're not listening to me.
你沒聽我說話。

A What shall I do?
我應該怎麼辦？

B You're not listening to me.
你沒聽我說話。

A What do you think?
你覺得呢？

B You're not listening to me.
你沒聽我說話。

A I'm so confused.
我好疑惑喔！

B You're not listening to me.
你沒聽我說話。

Are you done?

你說完了嗎？你吃完了嗎？你做完了嗎？

A	Are you done? 你説完了嗎？
B	**You're not listening to me.** 你沒聽我説話。
A	Hello? 你有在聽嗎？
B	Are you done? 你説完了嗎？
A	Are you done? 你説完了嗎？
B	**Are you listening?** 你有在聽嗎？
A	Are you done? 你説完了嗎？
B	**What do you think?** 你覺得呢？
A	Are you done? 你吃完了嗎？
B	**Yes, I am.** 是的，我吃完了。
A	Are you done? 你吃完了嗎？
B	**No, not yet.** 沒有，我還沒吃完。

You are telling me.

還用得著你來告訴我嗎？

A Hey, you look terrible.
嘿，你看起來糟透了！

B You are telling me.
還用得著你來告訴我嗎？

A Your girlfriend is seeing someone else.
你的女朋友和別人交往中。

B You are telling me.
還用得著你來告訴我嗎？

A David is not your Mr. Right
大衛不是你的真命天子。

B You are telling me.
還用得著你來告訴我嗎？

A I would say you made a mistake.
我覺得你犯了個錯誤。

B You are telling me.
還用得著你來告訴我嗎？

A Don't you think it's your fault?
你不覺得是你的錯？

B You are telling me.
還用得著你來告訴我嗎？

A You didn't pass your exam, did you?
你考壞了，對吧？

B You are telling me.
還用得著你來告訴我嗎？

I'll see what I can do.

我看看能幫什麼忙。

A Can you help me?
你可以幫我忙嗎？

B I'll see what I can do.
我看看能幫什麼忙。

A Can you help me with this?
可以幫我一下這個嗎？

B I'll see what I can do.
我看看能幫什麼忙。

A Do something.
想想辦法吧！

B I'll see what I can do.
我看看能幫什麼忙。

A What are you going to do?
你要做什麼？

B I'll see what I can do.
我看看能幫什麼忙。

A What's your idea?
你有什麼想法呢？

B I'll see what I can do.
我看看能幫什麼忙。

A My phone was out of order.
我的電話壞了！

B I'll see what I can do.
我看看能幫什麼忙。

What do you do for fun?

你有什麼嗜好？

A What do you do for fun?
你有什麼嗜好？

B I play games.
我玩遊戲。

A What do you do for fun?
你有什麼嗜好？

B I enjoy listening to the music.
我喜歡聽音樂。

A What do you do for fun?
你有什麼嗜好？

B I like swimming.
我喜歡游泳。

A What do you do for fun?
你有什麼嗜好？

B I go camping with my family.
我和家人去露營。

A What do you do for fun?
你有什麼嗜好？

B I usually go fishing with my father.
我通常和我父親去釣魚。

A What do you do for fun?
你有什麼嗜好？

B I like a lot of stuff: bicycles, rock climbing and camping.
我喜歡很多東西：騎腳踏車、攀岩和露營。

You never know.

很難說！/有可能！

A	Do you think he will be back? 你覺得他會回來嗎？
B	You never know. 很難說！
A	Can you make it? 你辦得到嗎？
B	You never know. 很難說！
A	Will she arrive in Paris on time? 她會準時到達巴黎嗎？
B	You never know. 很難說！
A	Is it possible? 可能嗎？
B	You never know. 很難說！
A	Did I do something wrong? 我有做錯事嗎？
B	You never know. 很難說！
A	What are we gonna get? 我們要拿什麼？
B	You never know. 很難說！

You can take it from me.

你可以相信我的話。

A You promise?
你保證？

B You can take it from me.
你可以相信我的話。

A Is that true?
是事實嗎？

B You can take it from me.
你可以相信我的話。

A I can't believe it.
我真是不敢相信。

B You can take it from me.
你可以相信我的話。

A It can't be.
不會吧！

B You can take it from me.
你可以相信我的話。

A It's impossible.
不可能！

B You can take it from me.
你可以相信我的話。

A Are you sure?
你確定？

B You can take it from me.
你可以相信我的話。

Spit it out.

話要說出來!(話不要悶在心裡!)

A	**Listen, I..., uh....** 聽著,我…嗯…
B	Hey, you wanna say something? Spit it out! 嘿,你想要說什麼嗎?說出來吧!
A	**I don't know what to say.** 我不知道要說什麼。
B	Spit it out. 話要說出來!
A	**It's so embarrassed.** 真是丟臉!
B	Spit it out. 話要說出來!
A	**Should I tell her?** 我應該告訴她嗎?
B	You know what? Just spit it out. 你知道嗎?就把話說出來!
A	**What shall I do?** 我應該怎麼辦?
B	Spit it out. 話要說出來!
A	**I'm so nervous.** 我好緊張。
B	Just spit it out. 話要說出來!

Mind your own business.

別多管閒事。

A You shouldn't do it.
你不應該做這件事。

B Mind your own business.
別多管閒事。

A Why don't you just give her a call?
你為什麼不乾脆打電話給她？

B Mind your own business.
別多管閒事。

A I think you shouldn't give up.
我覺得你不應該放棄。

B Mind your own business.
別多管閒事。

A Take my advice.
聽我的建議。

B Mind your own business.
別多管閒事。

A Are you gonna apologize to her?
你要向她道歉嗎？

B Mind your own business.
別多管閒事。

A It's good for you.
對你是好的。

B Mind your own business.
別多管閒事。

Give me a break!

饒了我吧！

A I am really mad at you.
我真的很氣你。

B Give me a break!
饒了我吧！

A Leave me alone.
不要管我！

B Give me a break!
饒了我吧！

A I want those cookies right now.
我現在就要那些餅乾。

B Give me a break!
饒了我吧！

A Aren't you coming with me?
你不和我一起來嗎？

B Give me a break!
饒了我吧！

A Why don't you pick her up on your way home?
你為什麼不在回家的路上順道去接她？

B Give me a break!
饒了我吧！

A Let's go shopping.
走，我們去逛街。

B Right now? Give me a break!
現在？饒了我吧！

I will do my best.

我會盡力。

A Can you do it for me?
你可以幫我做嗎？

B I will do my best.
我會盡力。

A What will you do?
你會做什麼？

B I will do my best.
我會盡力。

A Try to find it out.
試著找出來。

B I will do my best.
我會盡力。

A Don't give up. Keep going.
不要放棄。繼續(努力)。

B I will do my best.
我會盡力。

A Aren't you going to finish it on time?
你沒有要準時完成嗎？

B I will do my best.
我會盡力。

A Anything you can do?
你有什麼可以做的嗎？

B I will do my best.
我會盡力。

What brings you to Taipei?

什麼風把你吹來台北？

A What brings you to Taipei?
什麼風把你吹來台北？

B I am here to visit my friends.
我來探望我朋友。

A What brings you to Taipei?
什麼風把你吹來台北？

B I am here on business.
我來這裡出差的。

A What brings you to Taipei?
什麼風把你吹來台北？

B I just moved back last month.
我上個月才搬回來的。

A What brings you to Taipei?
什麼風把你吹來台北？

B I work here.
我在這裡工作。

A What brings you to Taipei?
什麼風把你吹來台北？

B I live here.
我住在這裡。

A What brings you to Taipei?
什麼風把你吹來台北？

B I came to attend my sister's wedding.
我來參加我姊姊的婚禮。

Part

7

生活短語

Excuse me.

對不起。借過。你說什麼？

深入分析

"excuse" 是請求原諒的意思。"Excuse me" 是老外經常掛在嘴邊的一句話，代表的意思相當多。例如，要請對方「借過讓路」時，就說 "Excuse me" 。而如果你要離席去洗手間，也只要起身時說 "Excuse me" 就可以。

如果是兩人以上同時離席，就要改成說 "Excuse us" 。

會話範例一

A Excuse me.
借過。

B Sure.
好啊。

會話範例二

A Will you excuse us?
請容我們先離席好嗎。

B Sure.
好啊。

After you.

您先請。

深入分析

這是一句請他人先行通過的客套話。老外是個尊重女性的民族，所以常常可以看見在電梯口男士請女士先進入的情形，這時他們就是說："After you"。通常"After you"是接住"You first"之後使用。

若你是和客戶一同搭電梯，也可以幫客戶擋著電梯門，然後禮貌性地請客戶先進入電梯及先步出電梯。

會話範例一

A You first.
您先請進。

B After you.
您先請。

會話範例二

A After you, Mr. Smith.
史密斯先生，您先請。

B Thank you.
謝謝你！

Anything you say.

就照你說的！

深入分析

是指同意對方提出的要求，有時也含有不情願的意思，特別是在被要求者只能「照辦、不得有異議」的情況時使用。例如每次我都要求老公週末陪我去大賣場採買家庭用品時，他總是會捨不得棒球比賽的轉播節目，又不得不從，然後心不甘情不願地說："Anything you say"。

會話範例一

A You should paint the fence tomorrow.
你明天應該要油漆圍籬。

B Anything you say.
你說怎麼樣就怎麼樣。

會話範例二

A Would you do the dishes?
你可以洗碗嗎？

B Anything you say.
你說怎麼樣就怎麼樣。

It's ridiculous.

真是荒謬。

深入分析

「一種米養百種人」，世界上千奇百怪的事太多了，當你發現某件事荒謬到甚至有點荒腔走板般怪異時，就可以說："It's ridiculous"。

就像前不久有個男人竟在他那話兒(penis)上刺青時，聽到這個新聞的人無不訝異地說："It's ridiculous"。

會話範例一

A You know what? David is a thief.
你知道嗎？大衛是個小偷。

B I can't believe it. It's ridiculous.
我真不敢相信！真是太荒謬了！

會話範例二

A I am going to marry David.
我打算要和大衛結婚。

B That is crazy! He is your brother.
真是瘋狂！他是你的哥哥耶！

It's horrible.

真恐怖！真是糟透！

深入分析

　　"horrible" 是「恐怖的、可怕的」的意思，當發生不幸的事時，可能造成極大的震撼及災害，或是某件事讓你覺得很可怕或驚慌時，就適合說："It's horrible"。

　　例如美國 911 恐怖攻擊(terrorist attack)發生時，許多曾目睹災難發生過程的人，事後就是用 "It's horrible" 來形容當時慘不忍睹的恐怖情形。

會話範例一

A　How was your trip?
你的旅遊如何了？

B　It's horrible.
真恐怖！

會話範例二

A　How do you like this movie?
你覺得這部電影怎麼樣？

B　It's horrible.
真是糟透！

It's very kind of you.

你真是好心。你真是親切。

深入分析

"kind" 是「親切的」，當你覺得對方是個親切的人時，就可以說： "You are so kind"。或是接受別人幫助的時候，也可以心存感激地說說： "It's very kind of you"。例如大兒子每次幫我到庭院澆花拔雜草後，他就會非常期待我能夠說一句： "It's kind of you, Jason. Thanks a lot."（傑生，你真好心，謝謝你。）

會話範例一

A
Let me show you how to use it.
我示範給你看怎麼使用。

B
It's very kind of you.
你真是個好人。

會話範例二

A
Let me hold the cup for you.
我幫你拿著杯子。

B
Thank you. It's very kind of you.
謝謝你！你真是好心。

I'm proud of you.

我以你為榮。

深入分析

　　常常可以看見這樣的親子對話情節：父母為了子女擁有高成就或不平凡的表現而感到驕傲，此時他們最常說的一句話就是："I'm proud of my son."（我以我兒子感到驕傲）。此外，像是我的主管也常常會對表現優秀的部屬拍拍肩膀說："I'm proud of you"。

會話範例一

A　I'm proud of you, son.
　　兒子，我以你為榮。

B　Thanks, Dad.
　　老爸，謝啦！

會話範例二

A　You must be proud of yourself.
　　你一定為自己感到驕傲。

B　Yes, I am.
　　是的，我是。

Be patient.

要有耐心。

深入分析

這句話可不是「當成病人」的意思，"patient" 是當作有「耐心的」的意思。"Be patient" 是安慰對方不要太急躁、要有耐心一點。例如老公就常常鼓勵還在學習當一個稱職投手(pitcher)的大兒子說 "Be patient, son"。

會話範例一

A I just don't know how to ride a bike.
我就是不會騎腳踏車。

B Be patient. You can make it.
要有耐心。你辦得到的。

會話範例二

A I failed again.
我又失敗了！

B Be patient. Just try harder.
要有耐心。只要再多一些努力。

Believe me.

相信我！

深入分析

你是不是也有這樣的經驗：當你在陳述某件事時，對方似乎不太採信甚至是懷疑你所言的真實性時，此時你就可以說："Believe me"，這句話就是要說服對方相信你的論調。例如同事就常常向他的主管抗議："Believe me, or you'll be sorry."（相信我，不然你會後悔。）

會話範例一

A Are you kidding?
你在開玩笑的吧？

B Believe me, I'm telling the truth.
相信我，我說的是實話。

會話範例二

A Well, I don't like it.
這個嘛！我不喜歡它。

B Believe me, red is always in fashion!
相信我，紅色總是流行的！

Bill, please.

請結帳。

深入分析

「買單」的說法看起來似乎很簡單，但別以為！買單要用任何和 "buy" 相關的字眼。"bill" 是帳單的意思，其實只要用 "bill" (帳單) 就可以簡單地解決這看似惱人的句子了。

此外，表示相同的「結帳」意思，還可以用 "Check, please" 表示就可以了。

會話範例一

A　Bill, please.
　　請結帳。

B　OK. Here is your bill.
　　好的！這是您的帳單。

會話範例二

A　Waiter, bill, please.
　　侍者，請結帳。

B　Sure. Would you please wait for a moment?
　　是的！您能等一下嗎？

Call me sometime.

偶爾打電話給我。

深入分析

　　在沒有 e-mail 之前，感情的維繫是必須仰賴電話的，朋友間得多多保持聯絡才能維繫彼此間的友情，當你和朋友道別時，就可以說 "call me sometime"。此外，也有另一種簡單的說法："give me a call sometime"（偶爾打個電話給我）。

會話範例一

A Let's keep in touch.
我們要保持聯絡。

B Sure. Call me sometime.
好啊！偶爾要打電話給我。

會話範例二

A Give me a call sometime.
偶爾打個電話給我。

B I will.
我會的。

Calm down.

冷靜下來。

深入分析

　　"calm down" 是常用的動詞片語。當對方在發怒或生氣時，你的一句 "calm down" 是勸對方冷靜下來好好想一想的用語，能夠發揮鎮定人心的作用。例如小兒子因為和哥哥爭玩具，常常會失控嚎啕大哭，我就得耐心地安慰他 "calm down"。

會話範例一

A　I am so angry about it.
　　我對這件事很生氣。

B　Calm down. Don't lose your mind.
　　冷靜下來，別喪失理智。

會話範例二

A　Calm down, sir. What's the problem?
　　先生，冷靜一點！有什麼問題嗎？

B　This is not what I ordered.
　　這道餐不是我點的。

Don't lose your mind.

不要失去理智。

深入分析

當對方處於極度盛怒的情境下,失去理智的程度像是火山爆發般看似一發不可收拾時,你就可以勸他: "Don't lose your mind" 。

或是當對方決定做某件事,而你預期這是會遭人非議時,你也可以事先用這句話規勸對方,含有提醒對方注意不要失去理智的意味。

會話範例一

A I really hate them.
我真的很討厭他們。

B Don't lose your mind.
別失去理智。

會話範例二

A I'm going to kill them.
我要殺了他們。

B Hey, pal, don't lose your mind.
嘿,伙伴,不要失去理智。

Forget it.

算了！想都別想！

深入分析

"forget" 是「忘 記」的 意 思， "forget it" 表示「不要太在意」，這一句話簡單又好用，雖然帶有一點不耐煩的意味，卻也含有欲言又止的意味。而另一種是勸別人放棄或不要鑽牛角尖的意思。類似「不要再鑽牛角尖」的意思還有 "novor mind"（不要在意）。

會話範例一

A What are you wondering about?
你在想什麼？

B Forget it. I don't want to know any-more.
算了！反正我也不想要知道了。

會話範例二

A I'm really mad at him.
我對他真的很生氣。

B Forget it, OK?
算了吧，好嗎？

Come on!

來吧！少來了！

深入分析

常常可以聽見老美將 "come on" 掛在嘴邊，"come on" 可和「過來」完全不相關喔！其實 "come on" 有兩種意思，一種是「來吧」、「走吧」的吆喝意思，另一種是「你少來了」的調侃、不相信的意思。幾乎是所有老美都少不了的口頭禪。要學好道地的美語得先學會這一句話喔！

會話範例一

A　Come on, let's go.
　　來吧！我們走吧！

B　But I'm not ready.
　　但是我還沒準備好！

會話範例二

A　He asked me out.
　　他約我出去。

B　Oh, come on. I don't believe it.
　　喔！少來了！我才不相信。

Cool!
真酷！

深入分析

    "cool"是冷的意思，也是老美年輕人之間的流行用語，有一點類似中文「酷喔」、「真炫」、「超棒」的意思，比較適合在非正式場合中使用。例如大兒子就曾經用羨慕的語氣說他同學火影忍者的裝扮："It's so oool"，另外一個相同意思的用法為"It's awesome"（真酷！）

會話範例一

A Look that new brand bike!
瞧瞧那部全新的腳踏車。

B Cool.
真酷！

會話範例二

A Look what I got.
看我拿了什麼！

B It's so cool.
真是酷斃了！

Count me in.

把我算進去。/算我一份。

深入分析

當一群人打算結夥去作某件事時,而你也想參與時,就可以說 "Count me in" ,例如每次我問誰要和我去購物中心時,老公和兒子們就會貼心地陪我去,他們總是會異口同聲地說: "Count me in" 。而相反意思「不要把我算入」則是 "Count me out" 。

會話範例一

A Are you in or out?
你到底要不要參加?

B Count me in.
把我算進去。

會話範例二

A Anyone wants to go with me?
有誰要和我一起去?

B Count me out.
不把我算進去。

Do me a favor.

幫我一個忙。

深入分析

　　"do someone a favor" 是央求別人幫忙的一種請託辭，是老美使用相當頻繁的一個句子，屬於非正式場合使用。類似這種口語的請求幫助還有以下的說法："give me a hand"，字面意思是「給我一隻手」，背後含意就是「幫我一個忙」的意思。

會話範例一

A
Would you do me a favor?
你能幫我一個忙嗎？

B
Sure. What is it?
好啊！什麼事？

會話範例二

A
Give me a hand.
幫我一個忙！

B
Sure. What can I do for you?
好啊！我能為你作什麼？

Don't mention it.

不必客氣！

深入分析

　　"don't mention it" 的字面解釋是「不要提起它」，但意思就是「不必客氣」，例如當別人感謝你的幫助時，你就可以瀟灑地回應對方："Don't mention it"。相同的「不用客氣」的意思還有另一種說法："No problem" 以及 "you're welcome"。

會話範例一

A Thank you so much.
謝謝你。

B Don't mention it.
不必客氣。

會話範例二

A Thank you. You've been really helpful.
謝謝你！你真的幫了大忙！

B Don't mention it.
不必客氣。

Don't take it so hard.

看開一點。

深入分析

　　舉凡勸人想開一點、不要鑽牛角尖、不要和自己過不去等情境中，都可以安慰對方："don't take it so hard"。例如當朋友被女友拋棄而自暴自棄、考砸了考試、找工作不順利、面臨人生巨變等，都可以安慰對方："Don't take it so hard"。

會話範例一

A　I can't believe it. She left me at all.
　　我真是不敢相信。她終究還是離開我了！

B　Don't take it so hard.
　　看開一點。

會話範例二

A　How could you do this to me?
　　你怎麼可以這樣對待我？

B　Come on. Don't take it so hard.
　　不要這樣！看開一點吧！

Let me drive you home.

讓我開車載你回家。

深入分析

　　如果你打算要「開車載某人回家」，在此勸你可不要自作聰明想破頭：回家是 "go home"，那麼「載」的英文又是什麼？其實「開車載某人回家」有習慣用法，你只要用 "drive(駕駛)＋人名＋home" 的句型，就是「開車載人回家」的意思，是不是簡單又好記呢！

會話範例一

A Let me drive you home.
讓我開車載你回家。

B No, thanks.
不用，謝謝！

會話範例二

A Do you need me to drive you home?
你需不需要我載你回家啊？

B Yes, please.
好啊，麻煩你囉！

Enough!

夠了！

深入分析

當你對某一個混亂的現況感到「受夠了」或是不耐煩時，"Enough！" 就是非常適合你心境的用語。例如兄弟倆常為了誰可以先玩電腦而吵鬧不休時，甚至變本加厲打架時，我就會出言制止："That's enough, you guys"（兩位，夠了喔！），表示希望他們雙方能夠馬上停止吵鬧。

會話範例一

A I won't let him leave.
我不會讓他離開的。

B That's enough.
夠了喔！

會話範例二

A Mom, David bit me again.
媽，大衛又咬我了。

B Enough! I have to punish both of you.
夠了，我兩個人都要處罰！

Go ahead.

去吧!隨你便!繼續!可以。

深入分析

老美使用這句話的機會真的是非常多,"go ahead"的字面解釋意思是「往前走」,表示「允許」、「隨你便」,也是允許對方「做某事」或是「可以繼續做某事」的意思。

像是大兒子每次央求我是否可以讓他在週六下午和同學一起去公園打球時,我就會說"Go ahead"表示允許。

會話範例一

A
May I go to the bathroom, sir?
老師,我可以去廁所嗎?

B
Just go ahead.
儘管去吧!

會話範例二

A
I quit. I can't finish it by myself.
我放棄。我無法自己一個人完成。

B
Go ahead.
隨你便。

★ 行動學習系列 03 ★

312

That's a good idea.

那是一個好主意。

深入分析

　　當我和一群朋友正為要去哪一家餐廳用餐而傷腦筋時，突然有人建議到某一家知名的法國餐廳，大家都異口同聲地說："good idea" 是一種簡單又常用的方法。此外，若是當大家為某個問題百思不得其解，而你突然有一個想法或意見時，也可以說 "I have an idea" (我有一個主意)。

會話範例一

A Why don't we try Italian restaurant?
　為什麼我們不試試義大利餐廳？

B That's a good idea.
　那是一個好主意。

會話範例二

A Let's call it a day.
　今天就到這裡結束吧！

B That's a good idea.
　那是一個好主意。

Good luck.

祝你好運！

深入分析

　　道別時總會說一些希望對方更好的祝福話，"Good luck" 好用又好記，就是「好運氣」的意思，也就是「祝你好運」，通常特別適用於對方即將有考試或面臨難關前使用。類似這種離別的祝福語，還可以說 "Wish you good luck"（祝你好運）。

會話範例一

A Good luck, buddy.
兄弟，祝你好運！

B You too.
你也是！

會話範例二

A Good luck to you, David.
大衛，祝你好運！

B Thanks. I really need it.
謝謝，我真的需要(好運氣)。

Got you!

騙到你了吧！騙你的！你上當了！

深入分析

　　先矇騙對方讓對方信以為真後，再告訴對方這是騙他的玩笑用語，有戲謔捉弄的意思。像是結婚紀念日時老公說要出差不能一起慶祝時，卻又突然準時回家還送我一束花時，他就說了 "Got you" ，意思就是：「你被我騙了，其實我早就有準備的。」

會話範例一

A　No kidding? How can you do that?
不是開坑笑的吧？你怎麼辦到的？

B　Got you!
你上當了！

會話範例二

A　Got you!
你上當了！

B　Hey, grow up.
嘿，成熟點！

Help!

救命啊！

深入分析

　　當你面臨危險時，「呼救」是重要的求救方法之一，但是身在美國可不要哭天喊地用中文大叫「救命」，那可是會叫天天不應叫地地不靈！一定要入境隨俗再加上使出吃奶的力氣大聲喊："Help"。

　　此外，你也可以直接而客氣地尋求幫助，就告訴對方："Help me, please"（請幫助我)就可以了。

會話範例一

A　Help！Help！
　　救命啊！救命啊！

B　Hey, what's the matter with you?
　　嘿，你怎麼啦？

會話範例二

A　Somebody, help!
　　來人啊，救命啊！

B　What happened?
　　發生什麼事？

I'm glad to hear that.

我很高興聽見這件事。

深入分析

　　"I'm glad to..." 是表示「我很高興…」的意思。例如當你聽見好友終於要步上禮堂結婚，結束王老五的單身漢生活的消息後，你就可以說 "I'm glad to hear that"，表示你同感欣慰，這句話也適用在當你聽見任何好消息時使用。

　　而相反的意思「我很遺憾聽見這件事」時，就可以說 "I'm sorry to hear that"。

會話範例一

A　I'm going study abroad.
　　我即將要出國留學。

B　I'm glad to hear that.
　　我很高興聽見這件事。

會話範例二

A　They are moving back.
　　他們要搬回來住！

B　I'm glad to hear that.
　　我很高興聽見這件事。

I'm sorry to hear that.

我很遺憾聽見這件事。

深入分析

美國人聽見壞消息時都會感同身受地說：
"I'm sorry to hear that." 這裡的 "sorry"
可不是「道歉」的意思，而是「遺憾」的意思，可以適用在任何不如意、會讓人難過的事件上。

相反的意思「我很高興聽見這件事」就是
"I'm glad to hear that."。

會話範例一

A I broke up with David last week.
我上星期和大衛分手了。

B Poor baby, I'm sorry to hear that. Are you OK?
可憐的孩子，我很遺憾知道這件事。你還好吧？

會話範例二

A My grandpa passed away yesterday.
我祖父昨天過世了。

B I'm sorry to hear that.
我很遺憾聽見這件事。

I can't believe it.

真教人不敢相信！

深入分析

通常適用在你知道了發生非常驚訝、令人不敢相信的人事物等事件時使用，例如發生美國911攻擊事件或聽見某個名人的八卦消息等，在知道的那一刹那，你都可以用不可置信的表情加上搗著嘴的動作說： "Oh, my God. I can't believe it" （喔！我的天啊！真教人不敢相信！）。

會話範例一

A　David and Maria broke up last week.
大衛和瑪莉亞上週分手了。

B　Really? I can't believe it.
真的嗎？真教人不敢相信！

會話範例二

A　Look what she's done to me.
看看她對我做了什麼好事！

B　I can't believe it.
真教人不敢相信！

I can't help it.

我情不自禁！我無法控制自己！

深入分析

這句話沒有任何艱深的英文單字，卻簡潔有力的表示「情不自禁」、「無法自制」的意思。當妙齡女子從你身旁走過，你無法忍受美女的誘惑而目不轉睛地盯著她，導致女朋友卻在一旁大吃飛醋時，你可以帶一點愧疚的口氣說 "I can't help it"。

會話範例一

A Maria doesn't like you, does she?
瑪莉亞不喜歡你，不是嗎？

B But I can't help it.
但是我情不自禁(喜歡上她)！

會話範例二

A My God! Why did you do that?
我的天啊！你為什麼這麼做？

B I don't know. I just can't help it.
我不知道。我就是情不自禁。

You tell me.

你告訴我(我不知道)。

深入分析

　　雖然字面是「你告訴我」，但是更貼切的意思是「我不知道，如果你知道，請你告訴我應該怎麼做」，帶有一點不耐煩的意味，也有反諷對方「你說呢？」的詢問意思。例如每次大兒子問我他要如何改掉咬指甲的壞習慣時，我就會說：" You tell me "。

會話範例

A How can you solve this problem by yourself?
你怎麼能自己解決這個問題呢？

B You tell me.
我不知道。

會話範例二

A What will you do to make her up?
你會怎麼補償她？

B I have no idea. You tell me.
我不知道！你說說看啊！

I have no choice.

我別無選擇。

深入分析

　　當一個人無法改變現狀又別無選擇時，肯定是無奈又沮喪的，此時就可以說："I have no choice"，表示「迫於現實的壓力，我只好這麼做」的意思。"I have no choice"的字面意思就是「我別無選擇」。例如朋友因為工作關係不得不常常搬家時，他也只能無奈地說："I have no choice"。

會話範例一

A Why did you do that?
你為什麼這麼做？

B I have no choice.
我別無選擇。

會話範例二

A Why me again?
為什麼又是我？

B Sorry, I have no choice.
抱歉，我別無選擇。

It can't be.

不可能的事。

深入分析

　　這是一句完全沒有艱澀難懂單字的句子，也是老美經常說的一句話，表示不敢相信或不可能的意思。

　　例如當你覺得某事的發生是「不可能發生的結果」時，就可以說："It can't be"。

　　此外，「這是不可能」的意思，你也可以用 "It's impossible" 來表示。

會話範例一

A I saw David leaving the house.
我看見大衛離開房子了！

B It can't be.
不可能！

會話範例二

A Maria is about to leave.
瑪莉亞要離開了。

B It can't be. She promised me to stay.
不可能！她答應我要留下來了。

It happens.

常常發生。這是常有的事。

深入分析

　　當某一件怪事發生的頻率相當頻繁，造成大家對此現象已經是見怪不怪的心態時，就是 "It happens" ，也代表「因為這件事經常發生，所以不要再大驚小怪了！」會這麼說就是表示只能接受此怪事經常發生的現象。

會話範例一

A
Look! He is so weird.
瞧！他好奇怪。

B
It happens.
那是常發生的事。

會話範例二

A
Check this out. Don't you think it's impossible?
你來看！你不覺得不可能的嗎？

B
It happens all the time.
那是老是會發生的事。

It's about time.

時候到了。

深入分析

這句話的運用相當廣，只要是表示「預期的時間到了」、「時間不多了」都可以使用。而若是表示「該是時候要離開了」、「該是時候作某事」時，就只要在 "It's about time" 的後面加上 "to +原形動詞" 的句型就可以了！

會話範例一

A Hurry up. It's about time.
快一點，時候到了。

B OK, let's go.
好，走吧！

會話範例二

A It's about time to go home.
該是回家的時候了。

B But I'm not ready.
可是我還沒準備好！

It's a piece of cake.
太容易了！

深入分析

老美說話有時也會用一些非常誇張的表示方法，當他們覺得這件事情很容易解決，一點也不困難時，就會說 "a piece of cake" 表示「太容易了」、「沒問題」。例如美女因汽車拋錨而求救於路過的男士時，男士就可以英雄救美地說："It's a piece of cake"。

會話範例一

A
Could you move this box?
你可以搬這個箱子嗎？

B
Sure. It's a piece of cake.
當然可以！太容易了！

會話範例二

A
Would you show me how to do it?
你能示範給我看如何做這件事嗎？

B
A piece of cake!
太容易了！

It's my fault.

是我的錯。

深入分析

當你發現自己犯錯了，就必須勇敢承認並承擔這個錯誤(mistake)，此時你就適合說 "It's all my fault"。例如每一次我發現家裡弄得亂七八糟時，不管是弟弟還是哥哥造成的，大兒子總是會替弟弟辯護而承擔所有的責任，他一定會說 "It's all my fault"。

會話範例一

A I was really wondering why it happened.
我實在懷疑這件事為什麼會發生。

B It's my fault.
是我的錯。

會話範例二

A Who broke this window?
誰打破這扇窗戶的？

B It's me. But it's not my fault.
是我。可是不是我的錯。

It's no big deal.

沒什麼大不了。

深入分析

當你覺某人的言行舉止實在是大驚小怪，就可以說："It's no big deal" 意思是「那又怎樣？」。

例如每一次我的一個男性朋友和網友認識當天晚上就會發生性關係時，他就常常說："It's no big deal"，對老美來說，似乎一夜情真的不算什麼。

會話範例一

A
David, you didn't do your homework.
大衛，你沒有作你的功課。

B
It's no big deal.
這沒什麼大不了啊！

會話範例二

A
It's no big deal.
這沒什麼大不了啊！

B
What did you just say?
你說了什麼？

You must be kidding.

你一定是在開玩笑！

深入分析

表示不相信對方所說的話，也認為這只是一個惡作劇或玩笑話時，就可以說 "You must be kidding"。另外，若是聽見對方荒謬的言論時，也可以說 "You must be kidding"。類似的用法還有："Are you kidding me?"（你在開我玩笑嗎？）及 "No kidding?"（不是開玩笑的吧！）

會話範例一

A I just got married yesterday.
我昨天才結婚的。

B You must be kidding.
你一定是在開玩笑！

會話範例二

A I forgot to pick her up.
我忘記去接她了。

B You must be kidding.
你一定是在開玩笑！

You can't be serious.

你不是當真的吧？

深入分析

"serious" 是「認真的」、「嚴肅的」，本句是試圖勸告對方不要做某事的意思，也帶有一點嘲笑對方「別做傻事」的意味。例如有一個朋友決定要去穿舌環時，一群朋友調侃他："You can't be serious"，類似的用法還有 "Are you serious?"（你是認真的嗎？）

會話範例一

A I've decided to quit.
我已經決定辭職了。

B You can't be serious.
你不是當真的吧？

會話範例二

A I went to see a movie with David.
我和大衛一起去看電影了！

B You can't be serious.
你不是當真的吧？

You bet.

當然。沒錯。

深入分析

認為對方所分析或所說的事「對極了」的用句，也含有贊同(agree)的意思，是屬於非正式場合較常使用的用法。類似的意思還有： "You are God damn right" 及 "You bet your life" 「對極了！」

會話範例一

A　I think David is going to Taipei next week.
我認為大衛下星期就要去台北。

B　You bet.
對極了。

會話範例二

A　Going to the party on Saturday?
星期六要去派對嗎？

B　You bet!'
好啊！

You are the boss.

你最大。

深入分析

這裡不但是指身份上真的老闆，另一層含意是「你最大，你說了算數」的意思，這句話帶有一點「無奈」、「莫可奈何」的意味，例如主管說今天一定要完成這份企畫書時，又希望你能幫他完成另一份評估報告，雖然他的要求不合理，你也只能接受，誰叫他是你的主管呢？

會話範例一

A　You have to finish it on time.
你必須要如期完成這件事。

B　Whatever you said. You are the boss.
就照你說的，誰叫你是老闆！

會話範例二

A　Are you going to send this for me?
你有要幫我寄嗎？

B　Yes, I am. You are the boss.
我會去。你最大。

You are telling me.
還用得著你說。不必你說。

深入分析

　　"you are telling me" 的字面意思是「你在告訴我」，但實際上，這是一種告訴對方「我早就已經知道此事了，不必你多此一舉告訴我」的回答，屬於不禮貌的回答法，使用時要注意場合，以免因為口氣不對而得罪人喔！

會話範例一

A　You are fired, aren't you?
　　你被炒魷魚了不是嗎？

B　You are telling me.
　　不必你多說，我已經知道了。

會話範例二

A　I think you've made a big mistake.
　　我覺得你犯個大錯誤。

B　You are telling me.
　　不必你多說，我已經知道了。

You're right.

你說對了。你是對的。

深入分析

當你認同對方的觀念或言論時，就可以說："You are right"，例如我和外子還是男女朋友時，我說的每句話他都說："You are right"。想不到結婚後這句話卻換成是我的口頭禪了。類似的意思還有以下的說法："You are absolutely right."、"You are definitely right."

會話範例一

A　I think Maria is so hot.
我覺得瑪莉亞是個辣妹。

B　You're right.
你說對了。

會話範例二

A　She is going to marry, isn't she?
她要結婚了不是嗎？

B　You're right.
你說對了。

You asked for it.
你是自找的。

深入分析

　　"ask for it" 表示「自討苦吃」的意思，帶有一點責難的意味，表示對方現在的所作所為所造成的結果，是要他自己去承受的，怨不得別人。例如朋友常常說他的妹妹因為放棄學業而無法順利找到工作時，就可以評論 "She asked for it."(她是自討苦吃)

會話範例一

A What did you say? It's impossible.
你剛剛說什麼？不可能。

B You asked for it.
你是自找的。

會話範例二

A Are you serious about it?
你是認真的嗎？

B Yes. You asked for it.
是的。你是自找的。

Could be worse.

(事情)可能會更糟。

深入分析

"Could be worse." 這是一種發表結論的用語。表示情況可能不太樂觀，甚至會更糟，是讓對方先有心理準備，接受這種不是太好的狀況。完整的語句是" It could be worse."

此外，也可用一般名詞當主詞，例如" Life could be worse."(生活可能會更糟糕)

會話範例一

A How did it go?
情況如何？

B Could be worse.
可能會更糟。

會話範例二

A So? What do you think about it?
所以呢？你的看法是什麼？

B Could be worse.
可能會更糟。

Part

8

常用問句

Can I talk to you for a minute?

我能和您談一談嗎？

深入分析

當你急著找老闆討論工作，可是老闆似乎非常忙時，你就可以趁空檔問他："Can I talk to you for a minute?" 通常只要提出這個請求，對方是不會拒絕的。相同「請求和對方談一談」的用法還有以下這一種："Got a minute?"（有沒有時間談幾句話？）

會話範例一

A Can I talk to you for a minute?
我能和您一談嗎？

B Sure. What can I do for you?
當然好！我能幫你什麼忙？

會話範例二

A Can I talk to you for a minute, Mr. White?
懷特先生，我能和你談一談嗎？

B Sure. Have a seat.
當然好，坐吧！

Pardon?

請再說一遍！

深入分析

　　當你沒聽懂或聽不清楚對方所說的內容時，若是照中文的問法：「我聽不懂你說什麼？你可以再說一次嗎？」是不是成了又臭又長的問句？在英文，只要說 **"Pardon?"** 就可以了。

　　相同的「請對方再說一次」的類似用法還有：**"Excuse me?"** 以及 **"Come again?"**

會話範例一

A Pardon?
請再說一遍！

B I said you should do what your mom said.
我說你應該照你媽媽所說的去做。

會話範例二

A Fill in the blanks with your name.
在空格填上你的名字。

B Pardon?
請再說一遍！

Could you give me a hand?

你能幫我一個忙嗎?

深入分析

這句話可不是要求對方「可以把你的手給我嗎」,而是請求對方給予協助的意思,就像是「提供你的手幫我忙」一樣,老美的幽默文學反映在語言上是不是挺好玩呢?提出幫忙的用法還有以下兩種: "Give me a hand." 以及 "Do me a favor."

會話範例一

A Could you give me a hand?
你能幫我一個忙嗎?

B Sure, what is it?
好啊,什麼事?

會話範例二

A Could you give me a hand?
你能幫我一個忙嗎?

B Sorry. I'm quite busy now.
抱歉。我現在很忙。

How come?

為什麼？怎麼會這樣？

深入分析

　　"How come?" 的字面意思是「如何來」，但其實是提出疑問的一種用法，簡單來說，就是「為什麼」的優雅說法，也表示「發生了什麼事情」、「為什麼為有這樣的情形」、「如何發生的」的意思，是美國人使用頻率僅次於 "Why?" 的常用問句。

會話範例一

A I failed my test.
我沒考好。

B How come?
怎麼會這樣呢？

會話範例二

A Maria and I broke up last week.
瑪莉亞和我上個星期分手了！

B How come?
為什麼會這樣？

How was your day?

你今天過得如何？

深入分析

簡單的問候語有很多種，"How was your day?" 就是一句使用率相當頻繁的問候語，看似簡單一句話，問候、關心的目的相當明顯。例如先生下班回家、兒子放學回家時，你就可以問："How was your day?" 甚至在家人共進晚餐時，也可以被使用來關心家人的一句問候。

會話範例一

A How was your day?
你今天過得如何？

B My day went pretty well.
我今天過得很好。

會話範例二

A How was your day?
你今天過得如何？

B Pretty good.
還不錯！

How did it go?

事情都順利吧？

深入分析

　　問候對方好不好有很多種方法，不要老是只會說 "How are you?" 這種公式化句子，偶爾也可以說 "How did it go?" 意思是對方也許正在從事某件事，你關心進行得如何？是否順利？

　　例如你知道好朋友去做身體檢查時，你就可以問："How did it go?"

會話範例一

A How did it go?
事情都順利吧？

B Terrible! I didn't finish my report in time.
糟透了！我沒有及時完成我的報告。

會話範例二

A How did it go, Maria?
瑪莉亞，事情都順利吧？

B Everything went well.
一切順利。

How's it been going?

近來如何？

深入分析

老美問候的方式有好多種，"How's it been going?" 是指「你近來好嗎？」的意思，通常適用在有好一陣子沒有見面的朋友之間，至於「好一陣子」是指多久則沒有一定的限制，只要是你覺得有一陣子沒有聽到對方的消息時，都可以使用 "How's it been going?" 的問句。

會話範例一

A How's it been going, David?
大衛，近來好嗎？

B Not very well. I got divorced last month.
不太順利。我上個月離婚了。

會話範例二

A How's it been going?
近來好嗎？

B Everything is fine.
都不錯。

In or out?

你要不要參加？

深入分析

　　當你要邀請朋友參加大家現在正討論的活動時，你該如何開口邀約？ "In or out?" 就是一個非常適合的問句，是老美年輕人間常使用的問法，屬於非正式場合使用。特別說明的是，不管是正常的交際活動或是見不得人的壞勾當，都可以用 "In or out?" 這句話來邀約。

會話範例一

A In or out?
你要不要參加？

B OK, I will go.
好，我會去。

會話範例二

A In or out?
你要不要參加？

B Count me in.
把我算進去。

Is that so?

真有那麼回事嗎?

深入分析

當有人吹牛說曾經和影星妮可基曼共進晚餐時,你就可以回應: "Is that so?" 表示吃驚、不敢相信的意思,是指「真像你所說的嗎?我不太相信」的意思。帶有一些不置可否甚至是調侃的意味。例如兒子老是抱怨同學可以每天上網玩線上遊戲時,我就會反問: "Is that so?"

會話範例一

A The singer Eminem is coming to Taiwan next week.
歌手痞子阿姆下星期要來台灣。

B Is that so? I thought it's a joke.
真有那麼回事嗎?我以為那是一個玩笑話。

會話範例二

A He promised to marry me.
他答應要娶我了。

B Is that so? I don't believe it.
真有那麼回事嗎?我不相信。

Are you serious?

你是認真的嗎？

深入分析

　　"serious" 表示「認真的」、「嚴肅的」的意思。"Are you serious?" 是詢問對方是否是嚴肅而認真的看法，通常會這麼問的人表示是帶有「此事當真」的疑問態度。例如當我聽到同事寧願放棄高薪的醫師工作而選擇到非洲當醫療團的義工 (volunteer) 時，我就問了他："Are you serious?"。此外，也可以在 serious 後有再加上 "about"，表示「關於某事是否為認真的？」。

會話範例一

A　I'm going to marry Maria.
　　我要和瑪莉亞結婚。

B　Are you serious?
　　你是認真的嗎？

會話範例二

A　I'm going to quit.
　　我要離職。

B　Are you serious about it?
　　你對這件事是認真的嗎？

What's the problem?
有什麼問題嗎？

深入分析

　　這是一種老美經常使用的問句，例如當警察發現一群人聚在一起時，依其專業的敏感度，一定會覺得事有蹊翹，通常他們就會問："What's the problem?"。

　　類似這種基本關心的詢問句還有以下的說法："What's wrong?" 或是 "What's the matter?"

會話範例一

A What's the problem, David?
大衛，有什麼問題嗎？

B I don't feel well.
我覺得不舒服。

會話範例二

A What's the problem?
有什麼問題嗎？

B Nothing happened.
沒事啊！

What's up?

怎麼了？什麼事？近來可好？

深入分析

　　若是想說道地的美語，這一句 "What's up?" 不可不知。"What's up?" 可以泛指「怎麼了？」「有什麼事？」「近來可好？」的意思，是老美年輕人經常使用的句子。有時 "What's up?" 也不一定是詢問你的現況，而是隨口打招呼的意思，要依據當時的情境解釋。

會話範例一

A　Hey, what's up now?
　　嘿，現在怎麼樣？

B　Check this out.
　　你來看一下這個。

會話範例二

A　Hey, David, got a minute?
　　嘿，大衛，有空嗎？

B　Sure. What's up?
　　當然有啊！有事嗎？

What's the matter with you?

你怎麼了?

深入分析

　　當你要詢問特定人發生何事時,"What's the matter with + 某人?"是非常適合的句型。某人可以用人稱代名詞表示,例如,若是你要關心對象是David,則為"What's the matter with David?"。此外,若是不指出姓名的第三者,女性用"her",男性則用"him"替換。

會話範例一

A What's the matter with you?
你怎麼了?

B It's Jack. He hit me a hard blow.
是傑克,他打了我一記耳光。

會話範例二

A What's the matter with him?
他怎麼了?

B He just broke his leg yesterday.
他昨天摔斷腿了!

Again?

又一次？又來了？又發生了？

深入分析

　　表示「事情又再一次發生了嗎？」的疑問句，例如我常常聽見大兒子說他在學校被同學欺負，所以那天他回到家又是一身爛泥巴時，我就訝異地問他："Again?" 表示我們之間已有默契，不用他說，我就已經猜到三分了，而我的意思是「又被欺負了？」

會話範例一

A It's David. He bit me.
是大衛。他咬我。

B Again?
又來了？(又咬你了？)

會話範例二

A He stood me up last night.
他昨天晚上放我鴿子。

B Not again?
不會又一次了吧？

And you?

你呢？

深入分析

　　老美說話不喜歡咬文嚼字，他們會捨棄冗長的句子而用簡單的句子來表達意思，"And you?" 就是一個例子，這是詢問對方的意見，通常是在雙方做過討論而也已經有人提出建議後，適用在詢問對方(或在場的第三者)的意見、狀況或建議等問題的情境。

會話範例一

A And you, sir?
先生，那您呢？

B I would like a cup of black tea.
我要點一杯紅茶。

會話範例二

A How are you doing?
你好嗎？

B I am better than good. And you?
我很好。你呢？

Anything else?

還有其他事嗎?

深入分析

　　適用於詢問對方是否還有其他額外的需要、意見、說明等。例如有一次我的一位朋友去麥當勞點餐,食量其大無比的他點了三個人的份量要自己享用,當他結帳時,漂亮的服務生還是職業性的問了一句: "Anything else?" (還要點其他的嗎?)

會話範例一

A I would like ice cream.
我要點冰淇淋。

B Sure. Anything else?
好的。還要其他東西嗎?

會話範例二

A I'm sorry that I made a lot of trouble.
對不起,我闖了那麼多禍。

B You should be. Anything else?
你是應該道歉。還有其他事嗎?

Something wrong?

有問題嗎？

深入分析

當你發現同事今天似乎鬱鬱寡歡時，就可以問他："Something wrong?"這是一句能表達善意的關心話，通常被問的人會覺得很窩心，會感覺自己被你重視，也是一句適合當成打開話匣子或開始聊天的關心問句。此外，"Something wrong?"也可以是在你發現對方明顯表達出疑問表情時，反問的詢問句。

會話範例一

A Something wrong?
有問題嗎？

B I locked myself out.
我把自己反鎖在外了。

會話範例二

A Something wrong? You look upset.
有問題嗎？你看起來很沮喪。

B Nothing. I just feel sick.
沒事，我只是覺得不舒服。

Are you seeing someone?

你是不是有交往的對象？

深入分析

當你暗戀一個女孩子而頻頻向她表白時，對方卻總是對你不理不睬的，為了徹底瞭解她是否已經名花有主了，建議你不妨可以直接問她："Are you seeing someone?"，這裡的 "seeing" 是約會、交往的意思，可別誤會以為是「你正在看某人」的意思。

會話範例一

A Maria, are you seeing someone?
瑪莉亞，妳是不是有交往的對象？

B Hey, it's none of your business.
嘿！少管閒事。

會話範例二

A Are you seeing someone?
你是不是有交往的對象？

B How could you tell?
你怎麼猜得出來？

Did I say something wrong?
我說錯話了嗎？

深入分析

有一次朋友在一個聚會場合開了女主人一個玩笑話，雖然他覺得無傷大雅，但他也發覺在場的每一個人都面面相覷，所以他就問："Did I say something wrong"（我說錯話了嗎）。所以下一次萬一你不知說出的話是否已得罪人時，最好小聲地問問旁人："Did I say something wrong?"

會話範例一

A What's the matter? Did I say something wrong?
發生什麼事？我說錯話了嗎？

B Yes, you did. You should apologize to him.
是的，你說錯了。你應該向他道歉。

會話範例二

A Are you serious?
你是認真的嗎？

B Why? Did I say something wrong?
為什麼(這麼問)？我說錯話了嗎？

Friends?

還是朋友嗎？

深入分析

當你和最要好的朋友因為吵架而和好後，為了表示雙方真的盡釋前嫌時，就可以問對方："Friends?"（我們還是朋友嗎），意思就是「吵歸吵，我們仍然還是朋友，交情應該還是存在的吧！」

此外，若是你要和對方「絕交」，也可以簡單地說："we are not friends anymore"。

會話範例一

A Friends?
我們還是朋友嗎？

B Friends.
還是朋友

會話範例二

A Are we still friends?
我們還是朋友嗎？

B Sure. I still care about you.
當然，我還是關心你的！

Hello?

有人嗎？

深入分析

　　"Hello"有兩種意思，一是打招呼，表示「哈囉！你好嗎？」另一種則是要確定是否有人在房子裡時，就可以大聲並用詢問的語調問："Hello?"。此外，若是和你對話的一方顯得失魂落魄或沒有仔細聽你說話時，你也可以提醒對方："Hello?"，表示「你有在聽嗎？」

會話範例一

A Hello, how are you doing?
哈囉，近來可好？

B Great.
很好。

會話範例二

A Hello? Anybody home?
哈囉？有人在家嗎？

B Yes. May I help you?
有的。需要我幫忙嗎？

Why don't you try again?
你為什麼不再試一次？

深入分析

提供建議的方式有很多種，在提供了許多建議卻仍不被採納後，就可以說 "Why don't you try ...?" 這是一種反問式的建議，有一點「乾脆試一試…」的意思。

建議的對象不是只有「你」，更可以將 "you" 改成 "we" 就成了 "Why don't we try...?"（為什麼我們不試一試…）

會話範例一

A Why don't you try to ask them for help?
你要不要試試打電話給他們尋求幫助呢？

B I just don't want to.
我就是不想要！

會話範例二

A Why don't we try the French restaurant?
為什麼我們不試一試法國餐廳呢？

B That's a good idea.
好主意！

Why?

為什麼？

深入分析

　　只要簡單的一句話，就表達了「為什麼」、「發生什麼事」的說法，是美國人常常掛在嘴邊的一句話。和 "How come?" 一樣！此外，若是否定式的問法，則只要在 "why" 的後面加上 "not"，變成 "why not" 即可，表示「為什麼不可以」的反問式疑問句。

會話範例一

A I really dislike Maria.
我真的不喜歡瑪莉亞。

B Why? I thought she was your best friend.
為什麼？我以為她是你的好朋友。

會話範例二

A I shouldn't do this to him.
我不應該這麼對待他。

B Why not?
為什麼不可以？

★ 行動學習系列 03 ★

Who is there?

是誰啊?誰在外面啊?

深入分析

　　相當簡單的一句話,可以聽見美國人經常使用, "Who is there?" 是指有人在外敲門時詢問對方是誰的問句。也可以說 "Who is it?" 以上都是慣用語句,但是可千萬別說成 "Who are you?" 因為美國人可是不會這麼說的喔!

會話範例一

A Who is there?
誰啊?

B It's David.
是大衛。

會話範例二

A I am coming. Who is there?
我來(開門)了。誰啊?

B It's me, David.
是我,(我是)大衛。

Where was I?

我說到哪了？

深入分析

"Where was I?" 除了是問「我人在哪裡」外，也可以是當你正在說話時，卻因為某件事發生或某個人插話，而中斷言論後，你要重新敘述之前的論點時，卻忘記說到哪兒，或偏離主題後要回到原來談論的主題時，也可以這麼使用。注意要用過去式語句。

會話範例一

A Where was I?
我說到哪了？

B It's about your family.
是有關於你的家庭。

會話範例二

A Keep going.
繼續(説)。

B Where was I? Oh, yes, it's about my job.
我說到哪？喔，對了，是關於我工作的事。

What's going on?

發生什麼事？

深入分析

　　當你發現街頭亂哄哄的，還有一群人在七嘴八舌的討論，你就可以問 "What's going on?" 意思是「發生了什麼事」、「怎麼回事」。或是你看見對方眉頭深鎖好像有心事時，你也可以這麼問，是表達關心的一種常用問句。

會話範例一

A　What's going on?
　　發生什麼事？

B　They are fighting.
　　他們正在打架！

會話範例二

A　What's going on here?
　　這裡發生了什麼事？

B　There was a car accident over there.
　　那裡剛剛發生了一起車禍。

What shall I do?

我該怎麼辦？

深入分析

　　當你徬徨無助、面對人生的抉擇，卻因為種種原因而無法作決定時，就可以說 "What shall I do?" 例如當女孩子面對兩位同時追求者，卻不知道該接受哪一份感情，或是想要拒絕男生的追求，卻不知該如何開口時，都可以這麼說以尋求他人的幫助。

會話範例一

A I don't know if you would get the job or not.
我不知道你能不能得到這份工作。

B What shall I do?
我該怎麼辦？

會話範例二

A It really bothers you, isn't it?
這件事真的很困擾你，對吧？

B What shall I do?
我應該怎麼辦？

What do you say?

你覺得如何呢？你說什麼？

深入分析

　　"What do you say?" 是美國人常常使用的問句，除了是問對方「你說什麼？」外，也代表詢問對方的意見：「你的建議呢？」通常是在對方質疑你的行爲或言詞時，你就可以這麼反問他。此外，若是 "What do you say to" 的句型，要在 to 後面加名詞或動名詞。

會話範例一

A What do you say?
你覺得如何？

B Yes, I'd love to.
好啊！我願意！

會話範例二

A What do you say to another cup of tea?
你還要再來一杯茶嗎？

B No, thanks.
不用了，謝謝！

What can I say?

我能說什麼？

深入分析

　　有一點無奈的意味，意指「我不知道該說什麼」或「我無法針對這件事發表個人意見」。通常是在無話可說的情境中，例如朋友常常抱怨自己的太太不願意煮晚餐，可是他卻又縱容太太提議去餐廳吃晚餐時，我就只能說 "What can I say?" 意思就是「你期望我有什麼評論？」

會話範例一

A　I think David should apologize to you.
　　我覺得大衛應該向你道歉。

B　Well, what can I say? He is your son.
　　這個嘛，我能說什麼？他是你的兒子。

會話範例二

A　Don't you think we shouldn't help him?
　　你不覺得我們不應該幫他嗎？

B　What can I say? We have no choice.
　　我能說什麼？我們別無選擇！

What can I do for you?

我能為你做什麼？

深入分析

這是一種詢問對方是否需要協助的客氣問法。不但適用在當你發現對方身陷困境需要你的幫忙，也適用在服務業中，例如侍者詢問客人是否需要協助的情境中。

類似提供服務的問句還有："Do you need any help?"（你需要幫忙嗎？）

會話範例一

A　What can I do for you?
　　我能為你做什麼？

B　Would you move this box for me?
　　你能幫我搬這個箱子嗎？

會話範例二

A　What can I do for you?
　　我能為你做什麼？

B　I'd like to check in.
　　我要辦理報到！

So what?

那又怎麼樣？

深入分析

這句話含有極度挑釁的意思，表示「你能奈我如何？」的意思，例如你不認同對方的所發表的結論或言論時，你就可以質疑對方："So what?"

此外，"So what?" 也是詢問對方「究竟該如何解決」之意，有刺激對方提出更好建議的傾向。

會話範例一

A
Don't you think you've made a mistake?
你不覺得你犯了一個錯誤嗎？

B
So what?
那又怎樣？

會話範例二

A
I shouldn't leave her alone over there.
我不該留她一個人在那裡。

B
So what? It's not your fault.
那又怎樣？這不是你的錯。

So?

所以呢？你覺得呢？你說呢？

深入分析

　　"so"是原本是「如此」得意思，但用疑問句" So?"在對話中使用，通常是詢問他人對此時正在討論的主題有何想法，或是不瞭解對方的意思而期待對方能繼續說明。

　　美國人說這句話時，通常會稍微提高音調或用誇張表情以加強語氣。

會話範例一

A I really dislike my boss.
我真的不喜歡我的老闆。

B So?
所以呢？

會話範例二

A So?
所以呢？

B So I decide to quit.
所以我決定辭職。

Do you have any idea?

你有任何的想法嗎?

深入分析

"Do you have any idea?" 是詢問對方是否知道某事的狀況的問句,是老美經常使用的用語。也可以當成詢問對方的意見,希望對方能夠提出他自己的想法或主意。可以在 idea 後面加上 "about..." 表示「關於某事」。

類似詢問對方意見的問句還有: "What do you think?" 或是 "What is your opinion?"

會話範例一

A Do you have any idea it?
你有任何的想法嗎?

B Sorry, no comment.
抱歉,無可奉告。

會話範例二

A Do you have any idea how much I should pay?
你知不知道我應該付多少錢?

B It's five thousand dollars.
是五千元。

孩子我們一起學英語！
(5-8 歲)MP3

為孩子創造最生活化的英語環境！一對一互動式生活英語，讓孩子與您一起快樂學英語。英語學習絕非一蹴可幾，每天 20 分鐘的親子對話，孩子自然而然脫口說英語！

商業實用英文 E-mail(業務篇)
附 CD

最新版附實用書信文字光碟讓你寫商業 Mail 不用一分鐘 5 大例句+E-mail 商用書信實例，讓你立即寫出最完備的商用英文 E-mail。

商業實用英文 E-mail(談判篇)

繼商業實用英文 E-mail【業務篇】後最新力作。你有寫 e-mail 的煩惱嗎？五大句型，讓你輕輕鬆鬆搞定 e-mail！

商業實用英文 E-mail 業務篇
(50 開)

最權威、最具說服力的商用英文 E-mail 書信，馬上搶救職場上的英文書信寫作。史上最強的商用英文 E-mail！三大特色：1000 句商用英文 E-mail+例句 500 個商用英文 E-mail 關鍵單字+33 篇商用英文 E-mail 範例。最搶手的商用英文寶典，提升實力就從「商業實用英文 E-mail（業務篇）」開始。

求職面試必備英文

附 MP3(50 開)

六大步驟，讓你英文求職高人一等馬卜搶救職場的英文面全國第一本針對「應徵面試」的英文全集！三大特色：三大保證：三大機會：成功升遷成功覓得新工作成功開創海外事業新契機學習英文最快的工具書，利用「情境式對話」，讓您英文會話能力突飛猛進！

Goodmorning 很生活的英語

(50 開)

"超實用超廣泛超好記好背、好學、生活化，最能讓你朗朗上口的英語。日常生活中，人們要透過互相問候來保持一種良好的社會關係。因此，只要一聲 Good morning, Hello, Hi!不但拉近你和朋友的距離，更能為自己的人際關係加分，英語小能死背，用生活化的方式學英語，才能克服開不了口的窘境！"

超簡單的旅遊英語(附 MP3)

(50 開)

出國再也不必比手劃腳，出國再也不怕鴨子聽雷簡單一句話，勝過背却派不上用場的單字，適用於所有在國外旅遊的對話情境。出國前記得一定要帶的東西：*護照*旅費*個人物品*超簡單的旅遊英語適用範圍*出國旅遊*自助旅行*出國出差*短期遊學…

商業祕書英文 E-mail(50 開)

商業秘書英文 E-mail**英文寫作速成班**?我也可以是英文書信高手！明天就要寫一封給外國客戶了，卻不知道該如何下筆嗎??本書提供完整的 E-mail書信範例，讓您輕輕鬆鬆完成 E-mail 書信

遊學必備 1500 句(50 開)

留學、移民、旅行美國生活最常用的生活會話！遊學學生必備生活寶典，完全提升遊學過程中的語言能力，讓您順利完成遊學夢想！

菜英文-基礎實用篇(50 開)

沒有英文基礎發音就不能說英文嗎？不必怕！只要你會中文，一樣可以順口ㄅㄆㄇ、英文！學英文一點都不難！生活常用語句輕鬆說！只要你開口跟著念，說英文不再是難事！

如何上英文網站購物(50 開)

上外國網站血拼、訂房、買機票…英文網站購物一指通！利用最短的時間，快速上網搜尋資料、提出問題、下單、結帳…從此之後，不必擔心害怕上外國網站購物！

出差英文 1000 句型(附 MP3)
(50 開)

出差英語例句寶典完整度百分百！實用度百分百！簡單一句話，勝過千言萬語的說明！適用於所有國外出差的情境。

雅典文化

雅典文化

雅典文化

雅典文化

國家圖書館出版品預行編目資料

生活英語萬用手冊／張瑜凌編著.

--初版.--臺北縣汐止市：雅典文化,民97.05印刷
　　面；公分. --（行動學習系列：3）
　　ISBN：978-986-7041-58-6（平裝附光碟片）

　1. 英語　　　2. 讀本
805.18　　　　　　　　　　　　　　97004476

03 生活英語萬用手冊

編　　　著	張瑜凌
出 版 者	雅典文化事業有限公司
登 記 證	局版北市業字第五七○號
發 行 人	黃玉雲
執 行 編 輯	張瑜凌
編 輯 部	221 台北縣汐止市大同路三段 194-1 號9樓
電子郵件	a8823.a1899@msa.hinet.net
電　　　話	02-86473663
傳　　　真	02-86473660
郵　　　撥	18965580雅典文化事業有限公司
法律顧問	永信法律事務所　林永頌律師
總 經 銷	永續圖書有限公司 221 台北縣汐止市大同路三段 194-1 號9樓
電子郵件	yungjiuh@ms45.hinet.net
郵　　　撥	18669219永續圖書有限公司
網　　　站	www.foreverbooks.com.tw
電　　　話	02-86473663
傳　　　真	02-86473660
ISBN	978-986-7041-58-6
初　　　版	2008年05月
定　　　價	NT$ **250**元

雅典文化 讀者回函卡

謝謝您購買這本書。
為加強對讀者的服務，請您詳細填寫本卡，寄回雅典文化；
並請務必留下您的E-mail帳號，我們會主動將最近 "好康"
的促銷活動告 訴您，保證值回票價。

書　　名：生活英語萬用手冊
購買書店：＿＿＿＿＿市／縣＿＿＿＿＿＿＿書店
姓　　名：＿＿＿＿＿＿＿　生　日：＿＿年＿＿月＿＿日
身分證字號：＿＿＿＿＿＿＿＿＿＿＿＿＿
電　　話：(私)＿＿＿＿＿(公)＿＿＿＿＿(手機)＿＿＿
地　　址：□□□
E－mail：＿＿＿＿＿＿＿＿＿＿＿＿＿
年　　齡：□20歲以下　□21歲～30歲　□31歲～40歲
　　　　　□41歲～50歲　□51歲以上
性　　別：□男　□女　　婚姻：□單身　□已婚
職　　業：□學生　□大眾傳播　□自由業　□資訊業
　　　　　□金融業　□銷售業　□服務業　□教職
　　　　　□軍警　□製造業　□公職　□其他
教育程度：□高中以下(含高中)　□大專　□研究所以上
職位別：□負責人　□高階主管　□中級主管
　　　　□一般職員　□專業人員
職務別：□管理　□行銷　□創意　□人事、行政
　　　　□財務、法務　□生產　□工程　□其他＿＿＿
您從何得知本書消息？
　　□逛書店　□報紙廣告　□親友介紹
　　□出版書訊　□廣告信函　□廣播節目
　　□電視節目　□銷售人員推薦
　　□其他＿＿＿＿＿
您通常以何種方式購書？
　　□逛書店　□劃撥郵購　□電話訂購　□傳真訂購　□信用卡
　　□團體訂購　□網路書店　□其他＿＿＿＿＿
看完本書後，您喜歡本書的理由？
　　□內容符合期待　□文筆流暢　□具實用性　□插圖生動
　　□版面、字體安排適當　□內容充實
　　□其他＿＿＿＿＿
看完本書後，您不喜歡本書的理由？
　　□內容不符合期待　□文筆欠佳　□內容平平
　　□版面、圖片、字體不適合閱讀　□觀念保守
　　□其他＿＿＿＿＿
您的建議：
＿＿＿＿＿＿＿＿＿＿＿＿＿＿＿＿＿＿＿
＿＿＿＿＿＿＿＿＿＿＿＿＿＿＿＿＿＿＿
＿＿＿＿＿＿＿＿＿＿＿＿＿＿＿＿＿＿＿

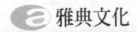